DELILAH'S
SHEAR DELIGHTS

By

Jon David
CUNNINGHAM

However great a man's
natural talent may be,
the art of writing
cannot be learned
all at once.

Jean – Jacques Rousseau

Welcome to my first novel.

One
Friday July 30, 1971

"Ladies and Gentlemen, again my name is Jacqueline, and it has truly been a pleasure serving you today. On behalf of our pilot, Captain Johnston, and all of today's stewardesses, along with Pan American World Airways, we wish to thank you for traveling with us. We would also like to welcome you to the Norfolk, Virginia airfield. For those of you who will be departing, I'd like to remind you to please use extreme caution as you exit the aircraft. Hold on tightly to the handrails as you descend the stairs. Ladies and gentlemen, the wind this afternoon is very strong, so as you cross the tarmac, please hold onto your personal belongings as we would hate to see you lose them."

As Delilah Mancini approached the exit door of the aircraft, she couldn't help but see the smile on the captain's face, a face and build that reminded her of Paul Newman. Then there was the effervescent and charming Jacqueline. Delilah jokingly thought to herself, how dare Miss Jacqueline resemble Audrey Hepburn so closely? Delilah was also positive that her husband of 21 years, Rico, had noticed Miss Hepburn's look-alike. He'd likely noticed all the other stewardesses, as well.

Delilah loved the sophistication and elegance of air travel. She was, however, totally exhausted from her day spent bouncing around in the clouds traveling from San Diego, California to Norfolk, Virginia. She wanted to find herself under a ceiling fan, in a cool dark hotel room, wearing nothing more than her panties and brassiere. That wouldn't happen for several hours as she, her younger son Nic, and Rico, had to wait for their older son Tony's flight to arrive from New York's LaGuardia Airport.

She wasn't sure if it was the lack of air conditioning in this small, antiquated airport or if it was a simple case of fatigue, but after traveling some 3,000 miles that day, she found it difficult to keep her head upright. Delilah truly believed that if she fell asleep, her family's luggage would soon disappear for parts unknown; or that's what her days of growing up in Brooklyn taught her to believe. Just as sleep finally overtook her, she heard a heavenly message from the airport's public address system.

"Flight 1017 is now arriving from New York's LaGuardia airport, at gate four."

Moments later Nic yelled, "Ma, I'm gonna run down and see if I can find Tony as he walks down the steps of the airplane, is that okay?"

With the unending energy of a teenage boy, he sprinted into the crowd, disappearing a few seconds later.

Rico yelled, "Nic, just stay outta everybody's way. You hear me young man?"

Delilah laughed to herself, knowing full well that Nic, like most male children over the age of six, never heard a word their parent said to them!

Rico gave his wife an adoring smile and called her by the pet name he'd given her in the early years. "DeeDee, my darling, how long has it been since you and I sat down with our boys? Just imagine, the four of us together for dinner tonight, it will be just like old times. I can't wait!"

Delilah knew that this day would come along eventually; she had always dreaded the mere thought of it. No, it wasn't that she didn't want to move back east. No, she and Rico had always said that when the time came for retirement, they were going to end up somewhere along the eastern seaboard. Her feelings of dread had nothing to do with coming back; it did, however, have everything to do with tonight's dinner. Delilah was just like any other wife and mother; she knew all the secrets and skeletons in the closets of her three men. Referring to them as 'men' might be generous, because there were days when they acted more like her three little baby boys.

Delilah often looked at the love of her life, Rico Mancini, and saw the silly grinning face of a skinny 14-year-old boy. Yes, he was the one she'd fallen head over heals in love with some 25 years ago.

That grin of his was so cute, but it was his eyes, the biggest and most beautiful brown eyes she had ever seen. They simply took her breath away! As time went on, she told herself more than once that it was perfectly normal for an Italian man such as Enrico Lorenzo Isaac Mancini to have a pair of wandering eyes. Yet, she had often wondered whether or not those eyes of his had led any of his other body parts astray. If so, just how far away had they strayed?

Of her three guys, Nic, although not her favorite, was her truest ally. Nicky, as Delilah called him, begged her to stop using such a childish nickname, yet he knew with a name like Niccolo Rocco David Mancini, that Nicky was better than her using his full name. He was the youngest child, and appeared to be a very typical 14-year-old young man. However, having Albert Einstein and Salvador Dalí as heroes, was a true indication that Nic was anything but the normal child.

Emotionally it depended on the day of the week, or maybe the hour of the day, but his mood would very often change like the clouds on a sunny day. In addition to the phrases, cute kid or bright eyed, there were even the occasions, sad as it was, when some of the other kids would have called him weird, odd, or psycho. Delilah understood why her baby boy didn't have much self-confidence, and a lack of friends, but it was still more than enough to break a mother's heart.

Then there was Tony, the wild child, who was the apple of her eye. His full name was Antonio Lorenzo Reuben Mancini. Delilah could easily have called him naive from time to time. However, Tony would say naive was when his schoolmates told him they were going to be the next Johnny Unitas, or Mickey Mantle, whether they had the talent or not. Somewhere around the age of eight or nine, Tony realized his voice was already that of a baritone. He didn't understand how he came to possess such a mature voice at such a young age; he just knew he had one. Just shy of his thirteenth birthday, he told his mother that he wanted to pursue his career on Broadway and leave their home in Pearl Harbor to live with his Aunt Maria, in Brooklyn. Delilah just shook her head, and it took all she had, not to laugh at his dreams.

She used this moment, however, to manipulate the situation, and knew in her heart he would never be able to pull off the perfect bar mitzvah.

Delilah forgot to take into account that with a birthday of June 1, Tony was a true Gemini, and also a great communicator. She told him she would bring it up with his father only after the bar mitzvah service was behind them. Then she reminded him, that if he did move east, the move itself it would be his only gift!

Tony quickly reminded his mother that if she wanted him to honor her thoughts on Judaism, she also needed to do the same. After a boy's mitzvah, he was thought to be a man. As it turned out, Tony had no problem pulling off a flawless bar mitzvah, and upon completion, found his way 5,000 miles east, living with Maria in his new home.

Maria knew the family required everyone to have names like tongue twisters. So when Tony moved in with her, her first act of friendship was to shorten his name, by way of giving him the pet name of Lenny, Lorenzo simplified. Before he even moved in with her, Maria was already his favorite aunt. Maybe they were kindred spirits. Maria also became his legal guardian and pseudo landlord.

Delilah took comfort in the fact that her sister-in-law had some influence over him. As time went on, and his career started to flourish, she wished she could take comfort in where his personal life was at the moment. While many parents deceive themselves into thinking the best about their children, the wool had not been pulled over Delilah's eyes. While Tony had the talent to back up his career, he was the purveyor of the most angelic voice the city of Manhattan had heard in many years. Delilah truly feared his naivety would someday become his undoing.

Many of her real friends would tell you she wasn't a perfect human or even a perfect mother, but then again, who was? When it came to being a true blue friend that is where she shined. At the same time, those who were privileged to call her friend could tell you she had a few flaws, one of which was her constant daydreaming. If there is any truth to the saying, 'the apple doesn't fall far from the tree,' anyone could easily see where Tony inherited his ability to dream. Much like Tony, Delilah was with you one moment; next thing you knew she had drifted away, to God only knows where!

"DeeDee, is anybody in there?" asked Rico ever so sarcastically, followed by, "Delilah Maria Russo Mancini, please come back to us."

As off key as he was, he started to sing, well, what Rico might have very well thought of as singing.

"What, what did you say, Rico?"

"I was singing our song, you remember, Rita Hayworth! I was also saying I can't wait for the four of us to sit down to dinner tonight. Where on earth have you been all day DeeDee?"

"Oh, I don't know; I was just thinking about seeing our wonderful boy Tony. By the way, I love you Rico, but Tony truly is the only singer in the family, so let's keep it that way. Also, it's five."

"DeeDee, what do you mean, it's five?"

"Rico, more than likely it's going to be five of us at dinner tonight. Tony has a friend traveling with him."

"Well, he's bringing someone for us to meet, is he? If he's anything like his old man, I'll bet you ten to one she's a redhead."

With an older sister who thought herself practically perfect in every way and a younger brother who felt much the same, simply by way of being the only boy, Delilah learned early in life that any attention was better than none. She insisted on having the last word, even if no one else actually heard what that word might be! It was her grandmother who forever told her, "Speak up child, speak up, and by all means stop with the mumbling." After speaking up once too often at the wrong time, she went right back to mumbling under her breathe for the rest of her days.

"If I know your son, it's a redhead all right, and God knows I'd love to say a she," DeeDee went on to say, and yes, it was said under her breath.

Oh Tony, Delilah thought, why have you put me in this position? For the love of God, you and I speak almost every Monday afternoon on the telephone. What's with you, and this sudden and overwhelming need to see us? Why did you pick this week out of all the weeks you could have chosen to visit? I know, I'm a navy wife, I'm supposed to love the whole moving thing, and even with the navy doing most of the work.

"I swear this whole moving thing, is a pain in the tokhes."

"Honey, what did you just say?" Rico asked.

"I said you're still a pain in the ass. Old man, please for the love of all that is good, go get your hearing checked. Here comes Nicky, Tony can't be too far behind."

"Ma, the stewardess and the pilots just walked off the plane and there was no Tony. What do you think happened to him?"

No sooner had Nic asked the question there came a voice over the 'PA' system. This time, however, it was not quite such a heavenly message.

"Mancini, now paging the Mancini party.

Will a member of the Mancini party please pick up one of our red courtesy telephones located throughout the corridors of the terminal?"

Rico, said, "You hear that Nic? We're having a party."

"Good one Dad. Never thought of that before."

"Hello, this is Delilah Mancini. You have a call for me?"

"Yes ma'am," said the operator, "please hold on while I connect you. Thank you."

Before Delilah could get a word in edgewise, Tony started to tell her about his wild and crazy idea. How the two of them had managed to catch an earlier flight. And that they had been at the hotel for a while, he also told her he couldn't wait for them to hurry up and get over to the hotel.

"Ma, did you know they gave us connecting rooms so you, Dad, and Nic can have one room and we'll take the other one."

Tony's statement was the proverbial straw that broke the camel's back, and Delilah couldn't be held responsible for what flew out of her mouth.

"Antonio, remember this, I love you, but you are a self-absorbed young man. Please, tell me you've been trying to make contact with your father or me all afternoon. Even if it's a lie, go ahead and tell it to me anyway. Forget about how tired we might be. Do you think your father and brother have enjoyed sitting at this desolate, godforsaken airfield?

We got on the first of three airplanes at 6:00 A.M. Pacific time, and you got on your airplane when, at what time this afternoon?

I love ya young man, but do you ever think of anyone other than yourself? Just in case you didn't know this, not all of us get to dance and sing our way through life, or live in some kind of fantasyland!

You also need to remember; this is not a vacation for your brother or father. You and your friend will sleep in separate beds, at least for tonight, and Nic will sleep with you. Do I make myself clear? There's supposed to be a very pleasant restaurant upstairs, where we will meet the two of you as soon as we can get there. Kapish?"

#

Tony hung the telephone up on the cradle on the nightstand, turned to Andy, and panicked!

"Damn it, we need to find someone from housekeeping and get those bed sheets changed out now! We gotta get it done now; they're on their way."

Andy calmly walked over to Tony, placed his hands on his shoulders, and shook him back and forth like a rag doll. Andy then questioned Tony's fear, and need for his mothers approval?

"What's the big deal, why all the worry? We have always done it like this. One bed is for playing around, and the other for sleeping. What are you afraid of? Worried she will tell you it's not kosher to kiss a boy, much less fornicate with him."

"She's in a piss poor mood! She just told me that Nic will be bunking with us, and you and I, my love, will be sleeping separately, at least for tonight."

"Why am I not surprised?"

"Well hell, she's not always like this! I could hear it in her voice; something's not quite right in my ma's world lately, that's for sure. Bystra moy suka!"

"Hey, when I taught you Russian, it wasn't meant for you to throw it back at me!"

"Well, I am sorry for calling you a bitch, and telling you to speed it up, but you need to get the lead out of your zhopa, bystra, bystra, bystra!"

#

After hanging the phone back up on the hook, DeeDee slowly found her way back to the seats where both Nic and Rico were sitting. As she sat down, before revealing the gist of the conversation, she let Nic and Rico in on her newest epiphany about her son, the singer.

"Has it really been 20 years already? I swear there are those times when I can't believe I gave birth to that crazy child.

I swear there is a direct tie between his looks and his brain, my goodness he is so good looking, but there's no getting around it, sometimes he's as dumb as dirt, hell, most of the time."

"Please, please, please tell me he didn't miss his flight again."

"No, not this time, he caught an earlier one! He's been sitting around waiting for us to show up. He said he'd meet us upstairs at the restaurant. Or at least he damned well better be."

"Do you want me to handle it," asked Rico.

"Rico, I love ya!" DeeDee said, as she looked up into the heavens. "Do you want me to handle it, he asks. Oy!"

# # #

It's unique how family resemblances occur, both Tony and Delilah have the same body types, long and lanky. On the flip side there have always been those who might say, "Mama's baby, Papa's maybe." However, there would be no way for Rico to deny Nic as being his offspring. As a matter of fact they look alike, walk alike, and at times they even talk alike! More than that, when they became hungry, they both change from Dr. Jekyll to Mr. Hyde.

"I know, I know," Delilah said, "Rico, Nicky, the two of you need to stop giving me the evil eye. I understand if either of you has to go much longer without food, there will be hell to pay. The two of you would just as soon kill Tony, as to look at him, oh my poor little Tony."

"Your poor little Tony, what about me and dad?"

"I'm telling you, if it wasn't a Friday night, and so close to sunset I'd say, forget tradition. We could ask the cabbie to find us one of those new fangled drive-in burger joints. Then we could just go to the room, and fall asleep. Oh, that sounds so tempting, doesn't it?"

"Nic, go get the first porter you can find and come back here pronto. We'll just drop off the luggage in our rooms, and then for the first time in a long, long time head out for our first Shabbat as a family. Please DeeDee, remember it's not about being kosher, it's about being family."

"You say that now. Something tells me nothing about tonight will ever be thought of as being kosher!"

"What did you say?"

"Nothing darling, but I do wish you would get your damned ears checked as soon as possible."

As Delilah, Rico, and Nic walked out into the heat and humidity of the mid-Atlantic's late July afternoon it became obvious that the airport's air conditioning system was working, if not working overtime!

"Rico it has finally happened. I knew in my heart of hearts that someday you would drag me into the very pits of hell. I'd always heard they moved slow in the South, but now it makes all the sense in the world why."

There was a long line of taxicabs sitting curbside at the airport parking lot, so it was easy for Rico to get his family into one of them, and be on their way. It wasn't long before the cabbie figured Rico and Delilah were from New York, he just wasn't sure which neighborhood. Their accents had softened over the years. It also didn't take long for him to strike up a conversation with his fellow New Yorkers. The more they spoke, the smaller the world became.

It was during the conversation they discovered that they had all enjoyed their fare share of summers at Farragut pool, and also attended high school at Erasmus Hall. As much as the cabbie was none to happy to admit it, he had finished his high school days long before his fares had even begun theirs.

During the conversation, Delilah's maiden name slipped out, and the topic quickly centered on her family's restaurant. Russo's Family Italian Eatery, on the corner of Bedford Avenue and Erasmus Street, was, without a doubt, one of Flatbush's favorites. Many high school student's Friday or Saturday night dates started at the restaurant. Over the years it had become habit for most, if not all the school staff, to cross the street and grab a bite to eat. Delilah's Pop gave a nice discount to the school's staff, everyone from janitors to the principal, and that didn't hurt the eatery's bottom line. She confessed that growing up across the street from the high school she attended was no fun at all. For her, summer time was the only time she could get away with anything at all. To tell the truth, it was the only time of year when the restaurant business was slow enough to sneak off and find some trouble to get into.

"Wow! What a small world it really is." Delilah exclaimed.

"Speaking of small, what brings youse guys to Norfolk?"

"Well, my husband just retired from the navy, and he has a new job here."

"Have youse guys already found a home, or you still looking?"

"Oh no, we found a house on our last visit here."

"So, tell me my friends, where will you be calling home?"

"I hope I say it correctly, Ghent."

"Pronounced perfectly, but the question is, east, west, or somewhere in between?"

"I don't know, Rico, where are we going?"

"Colley and Graydon Avenue."

"Well, well, well, my neighbor, welcome to the center of Ghent. My wife and I live on Colonial and Shirley, any further east and Lord help us, we'd be living with all those poor bohemian hippies in East Ghent. Somehow that beats the hell out of living over in West Ghent with all those damned rich Jews. As you said earlier, not only is it a small world, but it's also a short ride from the airport to the Admiralty Hotel. Here we are."

As the Mancinis' cab pulled into the horseshoe-shaped driveway of the hotel, the setting summer sun whitewashed the look of the building. Delilah was instantly transported back in time to a Long Island hotel where both she and Rico had stayed on their honeymoon.

Before Rico could stretch his legs and help her out of the back seat, the cabbie was there to help her. He awkwardly grabbed their bags from the trunk and handed them to the hotel's porter, then walked to the check-in desk. As he slowly turned, waiting for a gratuity, it became somewhat obvious that one was not forthcoming. The cabbie looked at Rico and muttered, "My friend you do know that the cabbies here, like the ones back home, work for a tip."

"Sir, if this Jew keeps giving all his money away, he'll never be able to afford to move to West Ghent. Here's a life lesson for you. Keep your damned mouth shut from now on!"

"Mancini, checking in, you should have two rooms waiting for us," announced Rico, with the first signs of fatigue straining his voice.

"I'm sorry, Mr. Mancini. I'm seeing only one room. Hold on for just a moment, if you will, please."

"I swear to the good Lord above, I'm going to kill him. I will kill the manager of this hotel."

"Rico, be quiet. You'll do no such thing; you will however be as pleasant as you can. Do you understand me? That poor boy doesn't need some old man hounding him, so stay off his back!"

"I'm sorry Mr. and Mrs. Mancini. That was my mistake. Your sons have already checked into your other room."

"My sons?" asked Rico.

"You do have two sons, correct?"

"Yes, and here is one of them right now!"

"I'm sorry, but two gentlemen checked into one of the two rooms several hours ago."

As Rico and Nic walked down the corridor, it appeared to be the length of a football field. Both of them soon realized, as luck would have it, that their rooms were near the other end of the end zone.

"Mrs. Mancini, will your party be checking out tomorrow morning?"

"Yes, at first light, we are moving into our new house tomorrow."

"Wonderful, welcome to Norfolk. I'm sorry if I said something wrong to Mr. Mancini."

"Don't give it a second thought, my boy, no one has ever said anything right to that old man."

As both Delilah and Rico crossed the threshold into the room, they simply wanted to fall into each other's arms, then drift off to sleep. They were painfully aware that this was not an option, at least not tonight. Delilah, like a moth to a flame, wasted no time making her way to the hotel's vanity, and quickly reapplied her makeup. Meanwhile, Rico thought about a sports jacket, but opted for a simple polo shirt. As they continued to run about the small room primping, their last action resulted in them both smelling like the other person's cologne, a mixture of Chanel and Aramis.

# # #

"Tony, can you believe that spiral staircase?" Andy asked. "It looks like something at The New Amsterdam Theater, back when the Ziegfeld's Follies were still playing there."

"If you say so. I swear Andy, what is it with your love of history? You truly are crazy."

"I'm telling ya, this lobby reminds me of one of the sets over at the Winter Garden the year we met. You remember? It was when you were dancing in Mame."

The two men continued to reminisce about the first show they were in together. They both agreed they were glad that the choreographer had the hots for Andy, while the director was just gaga for Tony. Had that not been the case, they knew they would have never met.

"Hey Tony, Tony, it's curtain time. Now entering stage left is this evening's leading lady. Look at her. That has got to be your mother.

She's got the same long, lean body and you have her smile. I think she spotted you. Now entering stage right, this evening's leading man. By the way, break a leg."

"Antonio Lorenzo Rubin Mancini, you get your skinny little ass over here and give your mama some lovin'. You hear me, young man?"

As Delilah stood there and received long overdue hugs and kisses, Rico and Nic also stood there, yet they seemed to be at a loss as what they should do next. Delilah looked away from Tony long enough to turn to Rico. She yelled, "Enrico Mancini, don't be rude, introduce everybody."

As the Mancini family and guest rounded the corner, they headed to the dining room, where the hostess, a woman with a thick southern drawl, greeted them.

"How y'all doin tonight? Welcome to The Barn. Y'all ever been here before?"

Rico whispered into Delilah's ear, "Damn, she sounds like she was raised in one, a barn that is." Hearing this, Nic let out somewhat of a snicker.

"No, well like I said, welcome, welcome. Will that be smoking or non-smoking?"

They all quickly looked at one another, and then shook their heads indicating the answer was no. She seemed to have missed the answer as she prompted them again.

"Well, don't y'all all answer at once now? Something tells me none of y'all smoke, do ya? It's not rocket science, unless you work across the way you know, up the river up at that NASA place.

You don't, do you? Non-smoking it is then! Well, let's get y'all some seats. Mary Lou will be with y'all in just a few. Nice meeting ya, and honey, that's got to be the prettiest long red hair I've ever seen on a boy. It reminds me of my granddaughter's strawberry ringlets."

After everyone devoured the crackers and butter, and downed the ice water in their glasses, Mary Lou finally showed up.

"How y'all doing tonight, my name is Mary Lou. It's nice to meet ya."

Rico gave his order before the young waitress could finish her greeting.

"I'd like to have a bottle of Manischewitz basic table wine, and five wine glasses and please get them to the table as soon as possible. The sun is starting to set."

"I'm sorry sir, but the Commonwealth of Virginia will not allow me to bring any kind of alcohol to the table in a bottle, much less serve it to someone under the age of 18. But, here's what I can do for you, if ya like? How's about we get ya eight glasses of wine, that's two for each of the adults, along with an empty coffee cup. As my momma would always say, there's more than one way to skin a rabbit! How's that for y'all, and by the way, Shabbat Shalom."

The waitress didn't stay at the table long enough to get an answer.

"Delilah, did you hear that, The Commonwealth of Virginia. What the hell is a Commonwealth?"

"Dad, that one's easy," responded Nic. "It's an independent country or community, a self-governing unit such as Puerto Rico or the formal title of the states of Kentucky, Massachusetts, Pennsylvania, and Virginia."

Almost as if spewing venom, Tony rattled off some gibberish, sumasshedshiy mal'chik. Andy's accent had already alerted the Mancini's that he wasn't home spun yarn. His next statement was a true attempt at helping Tony out of the grave he had just dug for himself.

"Tony, is the heat, or the wine that's getting the better of you?"

There was no surprise when Mr. Mancini reminded his family what he had done for the past twenty years.

However, it was somewhat of a surprise when his next statement wasn't as sarcastic or as tasteless a joke, as his family members had grown to expect from him.

"Okay, young man," Rico asked, "How did you influence Tony to learn a second language? There was a time when learning Hebrew or Italian was somewhat beneath him."

"Well sir, to be totally honest with you, I can say, I have never heard him say those words to anyone before tonight."

"I was in the Navy long enough to recognize Russian when I hear it. Sumasshedshiy is one word I do remember. So why is it you need to call your brother crazy? Come on, don't be shy now, and spit it out!"

"Oh, nothing, nothing, not important."

"Tony my boy, somehow I don't believe that for a minute! Andy, do you know what my son just said, to his brother?"

"Well, yes sir I'm afraid I do."

Andy softly mumbled, "Wow, the things you will learn about your boyfriend when you're forced to play Guess Who's Coming to Dinner."

"Andy, I could be wrong here, but if you would be so kind as to translate for me. Tony, tbi durak zhopa."

Andy's jaw literally dropped, and then the widest of grins overcame him. Rico and Andy laughed together, along with Andy agreeing. "Da, da, da!"

Delilah and Andy soon found themselves engrossed in a conversation, leaving the three Mancini men to entertain themselves. The conversation between Delilah and Andy took off like a rocket; unfortunately the same could not be said for the gentleman. There was the brief mentioning of Richard Nixon, and Vietnam. The conversation found it's way to the opposite end of the spectrum, when Rico spoke about the Cincinnati Reds and the Oakland A's. As the evening progressed, the wine began to dry up as the dishes were removed. As Nic began to fall asleep at the dinner table, and his snoring grew louder, Delilah insisted the party should move elsewhere.

"Hon, honey, Rico, please take care of everything if you will, its time for all of us to leave. I'm sure the wait staff would love for us to go! I'll see you back in the room."

"Mrs. Mancini, may I walk with you back to your room? I think father and son need some time to talk, to be allowed to catch up with one another."

Delilah grabbed Nic's hand and pulled him up to his feet, afterwards the three of them left the dining area. The two Mancini men settled up with the wait staff and then they found their way downstairs to the bar. It was while at the bar, they said good night to kosher, and hello to several gin and tonics.

No sooner had Delilah, Nic, and Andy gotten back into the room, Nic crawled onto one of the beds and with his continuing to snore made it known he would not be moved. It was as Delilah went rummaging through her carry-on bag; she found a bottle of Vernaccia. When she showed the bottle of Tuscany's finest white wine to Andy, he grinned from ear to ear; having grown up in Europe, he was familiar with the vintage. Delilah poured the wine into the two small rocks glasses she had found in the bathroom. Andy took a seat at the little round table; the one that always has an ink pen and paper tablet on it. As the ever-present demon of awkward silence continued to whisper into Andy's ear, his restlessness caused him to asked the silliest question.

"Mrs. Mancini, do you think they put paper and pen on the table so people could make up a shopping list, or maybe to write a suicide letter on?"

"To tell you the truth, I hadn't given it that much thought. But why think when we can drink."

Andy rose from his chair and took the glass, then thanked Delilah for the drink.

He toasted with a raised glass of wine, "Nostrovia!"

He attempted to explain that it was to their good health. She stopped him mid way through, letting him know she knew what it meant.

"Andy, please don't leave so soon. Believe you me, Nicky's out for the count, and the boy's won't come back till the barkeep kicks them out. This isn't what I would have wished for him, but then it is his life."

"I'm sorry, but I'm not understanding Mrs. Mancini."

"Okay Mr. Petrov, let's get schnockered and all will be clear as mud."

With the last two rounds of the wine and not a drop left Delilah let Andy know that his boyfriend had loose lips. Andy gave her a look that said he truly had no idea why she was talking about Tony's lips. She laughed then snorted, then explained to him just what the phrase meant.

"Andy, both my boys where born under the sign of Gemini. As you may know Tony was born on June 1, and Nicky's birthday is May 31. So let's just say I've had my days with those two, but I love them! Now there's my son Nicky, and he's got a heart of solid gold, but it's twice as hard and just as cold. But my baby Tony, as talented as he is, he's as delicate as the wings on a butterfly."

"Yes, your son is a true talent!"

"A word of advice if I may. Nicky will someday rule the world, or at least be a winner at what ever he chooses to do. I fear for my Tony, he's as naive and gullible as they come. He tells me you love him, along with all that you have had to live through. I can't believe I'm saying this. I have no idea what love is to you. Don't get me wrong! You are not the first Russian I have dealt with in my life. It takes a hard, and driven person to survive in what was once your world. My husband and father are true Italian, but my bubbe was from the East, and she taught me a thing or two about real life. I know just how hard love must be sometimes. I love my boys, and if you hurt him, Tony that is, I just want you to know. Ya ub'yu tebya vy menya poniayete!"

As much as the semantic may have been off somewhat, her facial expression instantly put a sense of fear into Andy's very soul. He understood she had just threatened to end his life.

"Da, da, I did understand every word you just said, very clearly!"

After that Delilah sat down with a smile on her face, and told Andy she wanted to know everything about the day the two of them met. He told me it was at an open cattle call. I was told it was also the day he met his mentor Billy, and the pain in the tokhes, Donald.

Reservedly, Andy stayed and continued the conversation with Delilah. When it was over he hoped in his heart she was just a protective mother. However wisdom told him otherwise. This wisdom also told him to not piss her off, and never turn his back to her.

After Andy left the room, Delilah shook Nicky and told him to go change into his PJ's and get under the sheet. She laughed thinking back to the statement she made about her youngest son ruling the world someday. Funny as it was, right now he was nothing more than her fussy little boy.

She opened the window and turned on the overhead fan, knowing the room was never going to cool down, but then a cool dry room was never the point. It was the sound of the crickets chirping, and the hot, humid night air, that reminded her she had found her way back home.

As she started to relax, she thought about the fact that this is where she had wanted to be all day. With dinner behind her, a glass of wine beside her, and a good night's sleep ahead of her. Even with the wonderful wine, she was unable to turn her mind off. Being back on the East Coast, where everything began for them so many years ago overjoyed her. Delilah met Rico at Farragut pool in Flatbush the summer before their fourteenth birthdays. She'd already decided that she would someday marry the perfect Italian man! Actually, her father was a shining example of Delilah's ideal man. It wasn't his physical attributes so much as his personality that she found attractive. Delilah's bubbe, her maternal grandmother, found nothing right with him! He was too Italian, and was never going to be Jewish enough.

The problem grandma had was that dad was a twice a year Jew, much like the Christian who only goes to church on Christmas and Easter. Delilah's Dad attended temple on the 'High Holy days' Rosh Hashanah and Passover, and that was about it. Delilah can remember him saying, "That woman simply hates me, but I love your mama, and if that's what I have to put up with to be with her, so be it."

A noise from the people across the hallway brought her back to reality, and she looked over at her Nicky's face. Noticing he hadn't moved one inch from where he was when they got back to the room. As she glanced at the alarm clock on the nightstand, noting the time she returned to her reminiscing.

As for the day the two young lovebirds met, Delilah had heard Rico's version, more than once, how he followed her legs all the way up to her ... and then he noticed her fiery red hair.

Being a lady, she never spoke about how seeing him climbing out of the pool with his soaking wet swim trunks showed her that at the age of thirteen, he had everything a grown man might someday need. Yes, his silly grin made her laugh, and his eyes were gorgeous. It was however what those skin tight soaking wet swim trunks reviled; she hoped that someday she would enjoy that too. She also remembered, how fearful she was that he saw her staring at his body while he adjusted himself. She thought she was going to faint when he walked straight up to her and proudly introduced himself. Between the Italian name, those eyes, and his body, well, that was enough for her. Later when she overheard him talking to friends about preparing for his bar mitzvah, she knew he was the one for her. As she continued to reminisce, she heard the door next door open and Tony's voice. She knew Rico would be along in just a few seconds.

# # #

"Sorry, I didn't mean to wake you. Where's Nic? I thought he was sleeping here with us tonight."

"He fell asleep shortly after we left the table, and your mom saw no reason to wake him...."

As the reality that Nic wasn't in the room entered Tony's intoxicated brain, he lowered himself on top of Andy. He then started to gyrate his hips, and whispered into Andy's ear, just how much he wanted to make love to him. Andy was not swayed from the coarse of the conversation.

"Why were you so rude to your brother? You know a hand full of Russian phrases, and you called your brother a crazy little boy! Your family wasn't impressed, and neither was I."

"Andrei Maxim Petrov, moy comrade, I need you, I want you, I..."

Without the slightest hesitation, Andy continued with his side of the conversation.

"Your dad shocked me, that's for sure! He understands more than I would have thought. By the way, I do agree with him; you are an ass and a fool."

"Things must have gone well with your dad. Did you get to talk, you know, tell him everything about us? Or did you two just bullshit the night away?

I mean, I don't see any bloody cuts or anything. I bet you a million Rubles that old man of yours could kick your ass if he had the mind to. I can't believe you lied to me."

"What do you mean, I lied to you?"

"You told me you were the good looking one. I don't know, give your brother a few more years and the girls will be after him; also your dad, yum yum!"

Andy watched Tony, and got the immediate reaction he expected.

"First off, that's gross. Secondly, you're drunk, huh? You and my mom, right?"

Fearing everything that could happen, Andy chose the path of least resistance.

"She had the good stuff!"

"Hell, my mom said my dad has always been a looker, and in excellent shape."

Tony was avoiding the original question and Andy wasn't going to let this one pass. "So, did you tell your dad about our relationship or not?"

"No, we talked, but not about that. That would have killed him. He might have had a stroke or a heart attack. I can hear my mother now, you just had to tell him, and you couldn't wait could you? Are you determined to make me a widow? She would have been right. Besides, I didn't want to end things in a bad way."

"End things? What do you mean, end things? We just got here. I thought we were staying till the end of the week. You're not running out already are you?"

With Andy's last statement, Tony's whole demeanor changed. Had he been caught in a lie, and if so, how was he going to find a way out?

"We are. We are staying, it's just that, well, it's just that, okay I'm drunk and need to get some sleep."

"Okay, if you say so. Come on, get in."

"No, definitely not tonight. It will be better if we don't sleep in the same bed. Nic is the early bird and he'll be the one to wake us up in the morning. That's not my idea of fun, explaining to him why two men are sleeping together."

"Good night, baby."

"Good night."

TWO

Delilah woke up realizing her dream of keeping a true orthodox home was about to become a reality. She always thought that one day she'd return to her roots. Not that there was anything kosher about the kitchen downstairs in the Russo's restaurant. Yet the apartment above it, which was run by her bubba, could have passed any rabbi's inspection. After the previous twenty years, Delilah was definitely longing to return to a simpler way of life.

The first time Delilah walked through the house, she looked upon it with absolute adoration. The protective mother in her loved the fact that all three of them would be able to sleep upstairs. It was the housekeeper within her who was ecstatic with an upstairs bathroom. She knew two messy men would share one toilet that would be hidden away from the prying eyes of new friends who might be visiting from temple. Now, six weeks later, when it was time to actually move in, she began to have second thoughts. Not so much about the house being right for them. It was more a matter of did she really want her teenage son across the hall? Where she might hear God knows what during the night. Then, she realized the next occupant of the guest room wouldn't be leaving anytime soon. When Delilah heard another one of the hotel guest talking outside their room. She stopped her daydreaming and started knocking on the door between the two adjoining rooms.

"Rise and shine, my little sleepy heads. Throw your trousers and tee shirts on, and let's get it going."

Before they knew what hit them Delilah had them all in a taxi, and well on their way to the house. She tried to gently remind them what the game plan was for the day. It was when she saw that no one was paying her any attention that she asked the cabbie to drop off the two useless men who had massive hangovers.

Afterwards she, and Andy had the driver drop them off at the nearest grocery store. After finding her way home she let out a whistle, the kind you make by putting two fingers in the corners of your mouth. Within seconds the three Mancini men were front and center. In the real world Rico retired with the second highest ranking an enlisted man could achieve; however within the Mancini household, Delilah held the ranking of a fleet admiral.

Nic answered first, and was the only one to show up immediately. Followed ever so slowly by the two elder Mancini men. Not much was going to get done today and she knew it. If she pushed any harder she feared she very well could have a mutiny on her hands. In her mind if everything made its way off the truck and into the house that would be just fine by her.

For all their difference, Rico and Tony had several things in common, at least that morning. After an evening of building up camaraderie, they both had the worst of the worst hangovers. Secondly, they both agree that they could use a hair of the dog that bit them. Rico's biggest problem was that he had forgotten that an employee from the radio station had volunteered to come over and help. Rico was in hopes he would forget, and than the old man could find his way out of all the work.

"Rico, my love, I see the moving truck has just shown up. Please go out and invite the gentlemen in for breakfast. Tony, will you please go and help Andy? He's cutting the fruit, and I'll be there in just a few minutes."

As the men, including the movers filed into the kitchen, Delilah began to tell about the custom of having apples and honey to bring about a sweet new year. Andy reassured Delilah that he already knew all about it, as he too was Jewish. One of the moving men said he enjoyed learning new customs, especially after his pastor had just spoken about Dr. King, saying that the segregationist and racists made no distinction between the Negro and the Jew.

The two professional movers went about their work, carrying in two boxes for every one that Tony and Rico dragged in. The truly shameful part for both Rico and Tony was that Nic and Andy were also out pacing them.

"Hey Mom," Tony asked, "Where do you want this box?"

"How is it labeled?"

"Tony's room."

"So, silly boy, put it in your room."

"Mom, I don't live with you, so why would I have a room here?"

"Boy, as long as there is a breath in my body, you will always have room in my house."

"So, where is this room of mine?"

"If you walk into the guest room upstairs, you'll see a little half door. That's it."

"Ma, that's the attic."

"Antonio, attic, it's all the same thing."

As the morning passed, it was obvious that Delilah was becoming somewhat frustrated. After twenty years of being a Navy wife, you would think she would have learned to take it in stride, and accepted the whole moving process.

Along the way through life Rico had learned a thing or two about his wife. When she got to that point, it was best to get her out of the way. He insisted she put on her most comfortable outfit along with some good walking shoes, and go discover her new neighborhood. He told her to go steal from the west and then give it to those in the east. He gave her a hug then sent her on her way.

# # #

Rico heard a loud banging on the front door, thinking Delilah might have forgotten her keys. As he raced down the hall, and sprinted to the first landing, he turned on a dime. He saw through the opaque glass door, the silhouette of a large man. Thankfully as he walked towards the door he remembered the deejay's name.

"Well, come on in, it's Jim Dandy, right, as in Jim Dandy to the rescue?"

"That would be correct, sir."

Rico welcomed Jim into their disheveled home. He then went on to ask what his real name was and how he came by his on air name?

"My real name is James Beckwourth. My wife gave me the nickname, after the song from the late '50s. Long story short, who am I kidding; none of my stories are ever short.

Rico then insisted that James take his time, and tell him anything he wanted to. It was not that he did, or didn't want to hear the story; no he really just wanted a good reason to sit down for a while.

"James, you take your time, the work will get done by three much younger men, who shouldn't mind doing it."

"I take it you have three sons who don't want to do the work."

"No, Jim, it's more like... well, never mind. That's a story for yet another day."

"Well, far be it from me not to listen to the new boss." Jim chuckled, and Rico smiled.

"I'll try and make it short, but Liz, my wife, and I met ten years ago, in an old dilapidated bus station. Some days it feels like that life was a thousand years ago. I'll never assume anyone knows how it was here in the south, back in the day. It didn't take long for me to learn just how hatful some people could be. You see, I grew up in Denver, Colorado. My great grandfather had a bit of notoriety, and because of it, I wasn't seen, or treated by the locals as a black man. My great grandfather was Jim Beckwourth the "Black Mountain Man" and the "War Chief of the Crow Indians". Now I'll finish my story as quickly as I can."

"Are you kidding, you have my full attention now. I want to here the whole story now! Take your time."

"Okay, but know this, its more than an either second sound bite. You see, Mr. Mancini, I was ..."

"Stop right there, Mr. Mancini lives on Staten Island, to my friends, I'm just Rico, got it?"

"So, my great grandfather James way Irish. He, and forgive me for using the term, but one of his slave girls had thirteen children together. Great granddad Jim was born here in Virginia, and then moved out west with his white father. Jim married himself four ladies, two of them were Crow Indians, one was a Mexican lady, and one was a Black woman. My grand dad, Jimmy later married himself a Mexican woman. Believe you me it's taken me a while to learn all this. So, as mixed as I am, no one out West thought of me as black. It's never gonna be a term of endearment, but most people just called me a Beanner. Its what most people called the Mexican kids. Imagine how I felt when I came out here, to find out I was really just another nigger, and a black one at that."

"Wow, being Jewish, I thought I had it rough, but this isn't a pissing contest. So, please, back to your story."

"Rico, forgive me, but I've heard someone at the station make reference to you as being our new messiah. Being Jewish, I'm sure you've got more than your fair share of horror stories."

"Yeah, but again this is your story: so tell me the rest of it. Then we can go find a watering hole where I can get a hair of the dog that bit me last night."

"Okay boss, but the fact is I don't drink anymore. I've had way too many hangovers myself over the years. But I will show you where you have to go to find some. We don't have the plain Jane liquor stores here. No, we have ABC stores, that's Alcohol Beverage Control. Welcome to the Commonwealth of Virginia. Let me try and wrap this up then we can go and help the others before you have a mutiny on your hands.

Phil, who was my best friend, and whose folks were about as mixed as I am, told us about this movement that was going on down south. We soon enough found ourselves on a bus heading to Washington DC. Funny, but as dark as I am, and with Phil being whiter than a lily, we learned that is was a sin against nature for us to even be friends down here! My goodness you can't imagine how upset people below the Mason Dixon line were that two guys would be friends.

Not sure how his new boss would feel about his story, he thought about what he had been taught from childhood; the fact is that the truth shall set you free. If this was his only chance, he was going to tell one more person as gently as he could about the realities of life for some black men living in the south in the 1960s. James went on to explain they were called Freedom Riders. He knew had it not been for the grace of God, he wouldn't be here talking today. He went on to tell more of the ins-and-outs of the mission he and Phil found themselves in. He then brought the story around to how he and his wife came to meet.

"As protocol would have it, we would sit at any lunch counter we could find, and we wouldn't leave till every black person had been served. At any rate, the bus pulled into one of the many stations. I found myself sitting at the first stool and Phil at the second. That alone sent the little old lady behind the counter into pitching a hissy fit.

A moment or two after we finally got waited on, a goddess walked into the bus station's snack shop. She and a black gentleman sat down catty-corner to us, and I heard him say something no man should ever say to a lady!"

"I'm sorry to say I lost any and all composure I ever had! I forcibly escorted him outside and beat, forgive my French, beat the crap out of him. I ran back inside and told the beautiful Miss Elizabeth Jackson that she and I might want to be moving on. I gave Phil a look.

He threw some money at the little old lady, he grabbed the food and all three of us ran out the restaurant. Beth and I sat together 'till we got to the end of the run in Mississippi."

"If you thought people were hateful towards Phil and me sitting together while riding on a bus, try marrying a white woman from Virginia, then setting up a home. She had to choose between me and living in the neighborhood she grew up in. She told her parents we would return someday. The summer of 1967 we moved back, and have never left each other's sides or the state ever since. Now, I'm not about to say the rest of our lives have been a cakewalk; Lord knows we've had our share of troubles, but life can get better."

"Jim, I do believe you missed your calling. You should be one of those inspirational speakers."

"So, tell me, boss man, how did you and your little lady get together?"

"You must be kidding me, right? Well, hells bells, I saw Delilah for the first time at a public swimming pool in Brooklyn when I was just fourteen years old. That afternoon, I would have followed her to the ends of the earth if she had asked me to. Four years later, I followed her to the justice of the peace instead."

Rico's facial expression was a mix of joy and sadness. The memories were fond, but they also included regrets and missed opportunities for happiness.

"We ended up there just days after her eighteenth birthday, several weeks before I left for boot camp in San Diego to prepare for the Korean War. Twenty-one years later, I'm sitting here telling you our plain Jane love story, knowing full well that your story trumps mine, hands down.

Just a second or two after his father finished speaking, Nic addressed both James and Rico.

"With all due respect, and now that you two gentlemen are the best of friends, may I remind you it won't be long till the queen of Flatbush gets home. Remember, it doesn't have to be done right, it just needs to be done, or there will be hell to pay.

"Jimmy, that would be my younger and often times most outspoken of sons, Nic."

"Sounds like a wise man to me. We all know how the ladies can be sometimes."

"Not all of us. My older son hasn't grasped that one yet, but then I'm not holding my breath either."

#

At a hundred and four floors, be it rain or shine, day or night, The Empire State building was better than the North Star. When it came down to finding your way around the city. Everyone who grew up there knew to look for the tallest building and use it to keep your bearings. It was Delilah's first day in Norfolk and she had yet to find one building that stood taller than five stories. She didn't worry though, because she carried Tony's old Cub Scoot compass. She'd kept it even though he'd quit scouting after only a few months of starting.

By the time she got to the end of the street, she found herself wanting to join in with the little girls who were playing hopscotch on the sidewalk. As she walked, she daydreamed about maybe someday teaching someone else how to play the game. When she came to the end of Graydon Avenue, she realized a decision had to be made. Should she go north on Colley Avenue or south? Heading north her first discovery was Henry's Bucher Shop; next to it was Master's Drug Store. Then came a block with a few apartment building along with a parking garage between the two.

On the third block it would seem as if she had finally hit pay dirt. Eggs n' Things looked like it might be the locals favorite little greasy spoon. As she was passing by she couldn't help but notice there wasn't an empty stool at the counter.

Next was the smallest dry cleaner she had ever seen, to the point she almost missed it. The next building was without a Godsend. It housed the three things she would need the most.

Virginia National Bank. Even if it was Fort Knox, it wasn't safe till Rico said it was. It was right next door to Curtis's Barber Shop. Delilah knew when she got home the mission would be to get him up to go get a haircut, that way it would be his discovery. As she walked past the bank she was overjoyed to find herself standing in front of Hadassah's Delicatessen.

"Shabbat Shalom. Gut Shabbles."

"What? Oh, okay. If you're looking for the Stines, they are in temple. I suggest you come back early Sunday morning. Shalom."

"Who are they?"

The woman behind the counter appeared somewhat puzzled as Delilah once again asked, "Who are they?"

"Are you looking for the owners or not?"

"No." said Delilah. "What I am looking for is some good fresh matzos along with some hummus."

"How do you want it?"

Delilah was becoming annoyed at the direction the conversation was going, and didn't appreciate the attitude of the hired help. "Just like I told you, good and fresh."

"Here's an idea lady, why don't you try being a mentsh, and treat the goy with a little more respect. Mishegas!"

Delilah glared at the woman and as she turned to walk out of the store, she stopped turned back around and asked, "Did you just try to call me stupid?"

"There was no try about it, you understood exactly what was said. I mean really, you come in here with the thickest New Your accent, speaking perfect Hebrew. Then you're going to be condescending towards me. Lady, you're on Colley Avenue, not Lexington, you got it?"

"Touché, I guess I deserved that. Let's start over. My name is Delilah, and my family and I just moved into the neighborhood."

"I'm Betty and my sister is Wilma, who also works here once in a blue moon."

"Betty and Wilma, do I look that gullible to you?"

"No, you don't appear gullible at all. But I was making a joke about Betty and Wilma, that's all. No, my sister's name is Annie. Better yet, go over to the beauty shop next door and ask for the receptionist, Stella. She is the bigger than life redhead, with the beautiful smile. Tell her I sent you over."

Delilah cracked a smile, thinking that this was more like it, a typical welcome-to-the-neighborhood conversation.

"Also, tell her you're new here, and she will introduce you to the who's who of Ghent. Many of your neighbors got their hair done yesterday morning for today's Sabbath service, and those who didn't are getting ready for church tomorrow. Welcome to the Torah belt."

Everyone who's anyone goes to temple or church in this neighborhood. It's the best way to 'be seen,' if you know what I mean. Also, this is the best I have to offer you. It's yesterdays late afternoon batch of Challah, along with a tub of fresh roasted garlic hummus. I know you asked for motzo, but hey, it's midday on a Saturday."

"Betty, thanks so much for the hospitality!"

Although Delilah was enjoying the conversation with Betty, she had more exploring to do and wasn't sure how to get out the door without being rude.

"Wait a second, did you say your sister owns a beauty salon? I would give my bottom dollar for a good ole fashioned shampooing!"

"What the hell have I been saying? You haven't been listening, have you? Delilah, go do your window-shopping, then step inside the salon. Tell Stella you want the grand tour; my God, it is only one big room. It will take her forever, but don't say I didn't warn ya. She can even out talk me."

Delilah made one more attempt to leave the deli as Betty started in again. This time she winked and said, "Just remember, if you're not back by two o'clock, I have my television snack for tonight. I love hummus, especially when someone else has paid for it!"

Delilah walked half-heartedly down Colley Avenue and made her way back to the beauty shop. The only place along the way that caught her eye was a quaint little antique shop named Table Seven. It must have been that menorah in the window display on one of the tables that caught her attention.

As she entered the beauty shop, she heard the loudest, yet ever so perfect, imitation of Barbara Streisand's voice.

"Hello gorgeous! Welcome to Shear Delights."

Delilah stepped into a salon that was void of any color, or was it that it was extremely faded from the many years the shop had gone without an update. Delilah knew the place had to have been last decorated before Tony had been born. She also had to admit that the Italians could give the French a run for their money when it came down to overdoing the décor. The salon walls were covered with sun-bleached and faded French Rose wallpaper. A small waiting area was crowed with white-tufted velvet medallion- back armchairs and the reception room wasn't outdone by the styling area, with white and gold provincial vanities and ornate mirrors. The last bit of charm included double-sided sconces with electric flickering flame-shaped light bulbs. She bit her tongue, trying her best not to laugh. She then told the lady behind the desk that Betty had sent her over. Delilah knew it was Stella who had just greeted her at the door. Betty was right; this lady did have the biggest, most beautiful smile she had ever seen.

"You must be Stella," Delilah said. Betty from next door told me to stop by and let you know I'm new to the neighborhood. She also mentioned that you would be happy to introduce me to your boss, Annie."

"She did, did she? She is such a sweetheart, that is if you can ever find it, or was that her brain they were looking for?"

Stella studied Delilah for signs of a sense of humor, however she didn't find one.

"Well, you picked the right day to come in for your first visit, Saturday at noon, the bewitching hour. You know, if you don't make it in by noon, you'll be looking like a witch at the Sunday morning social hall."

"I am so sorry, but you must forgive those northerners, they run on a different clock than we do down here. Had you been here at 9am, I would have loved to introduce you to everybody. But on a Saturday afternoon in the height of summer, most true southern have already gone home and have had their first mint julep."

Delilah's head was spinning from not only the thickness of her southern draw, but also from the smell of the whisky on her breath. There are those who say New Yorkers have an attitude, but this southern belle could have taken down the strongest of Brooklynites.

"Ma'am, this is what I can do for you. Over there, to the left, at the end station is my sister Margaret. She and our older sister Beatrice once owned this shop. Margaret, Margaret! She must have her hearing aid out. I'm sure she would love to work with you. I can get you on her book if you would like. The lady next to the shampoo basin, the one who is wearing the light blue sleeveless top, she's Annie."

Delilah simply stood next to Stella as she pointed towards each lady, and then went on about the lives of the few women who were still there.

"Annie, this is Delilah, she's new in town and Betty sent over to get acquainted."

"Delilah, nice to meet you, my sister called and said you'd stop by. I'll be with you in about ten minutes. I've just got to set Mrs. Babcock, and get her under the dryer. Is that okay with you?"

"Yeah, thanks for fitting me in, I know its last minute, so if you can't get me in, it's okay."

As Annie was finishing up with her other client, Delilah turned back to Stella, and thanked her for her hospitality.

"Hospitality, is that what you came in here for? Well why didn't you say so? Would you like it straight up, or on the rocks? You do know we Virginians were the first to make the Mint Julep, and of course we only use "Old Virginia Bourbon." Those old witches from Kentucky think it's theirs. Oh honey, excuse me, but its time for me to start serving the drinks. The last lady just went under her dryer. I gotta get all the money together. Shove it in the coffee can, and then call it a weekend."

"Well after Annie shampoos my head I can start my weekend also. But then I guess I should get back to unpacking all the boxes."

"Oh hell, you poor thing you. Boxes! If I were you, I'd get the bourbon, food and toilet paper, and get myself through the weekend. Then and start the rest of the unpacking on Monday morning. Hell girl, come on back on Tuesday morning and get to know the real us, in a better light."

"Stella, I don't think it could get any more real than it is right now."

THREE

There are many businesses where comradely and teamwork are essential to its success. However, there is another one where hatred and jealousy are the fuel that often generates the best results. That business would be 'Show Business'. The kinder the words spoken about someone, the more likely you have stumbled upon their nemesis. Funny how many of the actors love to spend time in the sickeningly sweet labyrinth of lies!

On stage, however, when the lights are on and the curtain is up, it is pride alone that keeps everything in check. It is also because of that pride no mistakes were ever made. However, what went on back stage could be said to be where the true entertainment took place. Dance calls, vocal warm ups, and makeup calls, was most likely the time when the claws came out, and the venom was often spewed. If ever there were a time and place to have been the proverbial fly on the wall, it would be the same Saturday morning when both Andy and Tony were down south, on vacation. The place to be would definitely be just inside the stage door at 237 W. 51 Street in the Warner Hollywood Theatre.

"So Billy," Donald asked, "did they fly down or take the bus?"

Someone from within the ensemble yelled out. "I heard somebody say he didn't have the airfare."

Donald responded by saying, "I find that hard to believe. We are, after all, talking about one of the principles actors. The one who was nominated for a Tony Award for best supporting actor. The one who is rolling in all the dough.

You know, the man who, up until just a few weeks ago, would have bought everyone in the company a drink at the club every night."

"Donald for God's sake can ya give it a rest already?" Replied another one of the dancers. Almost as quickly as he finished, Billy let his opinion be known ever so loudly.

"Donald, thou dost protest too much. Funny how you've yet to tame that green-eyed beast, you know your jealousy knows no bounds, does it?"

"Billy I heard his folks moved to the smallest town they could find just so he wouldn't come to visit." one of Donald's little minions yelled out.

"I'm sorry, my little 'Maleficent', but are you actually speaking to me? Or was that one of your misinformed little puppets." Billy asked.

Moments later, another voice from the crowd rang out, "Billy, did you get a phone call from Sleeping Beauty or Merryweather this morning? God knows you can't stay out of their lives, not even for a minute, can you?"

Donald's razor sharp retort, "Look ladies, does anyone really care?" Certain he had made it obvious that there was no love lost between any of them.

Professional singers, friendly or not, are almost always competitive with others in their craft. As for acting, Billy had been playing on the boards, or running across the stage, for what seemed like an eternity. With the maturity of Tony's voice, Billy could have easily been intimidated, but Billy could hold his own, as an actor, with the greatest of ease. On a personal level, Billy came undone the first day he met Tony. There was no doubt that Tony was a 'pretty boy', but somehow Billy saw past all that, and saw the true innocence that was Tony Mancini.

Over the last four years of working and socializing with Tony, Billy's love for him grew, not romantically; no, it was a paternal love. Billy was the same age as Rico Mancini, and could easily look at Tony and see the child he had secretly longed for.

On that hot Saturday morning, while Billy was standing in line at his favorite bodega, it dawned on him. It had only been one show without Tony working by his side. How was he going to get through the next seven shows? Billy was already longing to see Tony again.

With all the cackling of the hens in the proverbial hen house, Billy was so easily distracted. He began to drift away and replay the events of his morning. He knew it was going to be a hell of a day when he got to the station and watched the train pull away from the platform without him. He knew he could have caught a cat nap, somewhere between New Rochelle and Grand Central, but he chose to sleep in for an extra twenty minutes. He liked being early for everything. The decibel level of chatter continued to grow in the dressing room, and suddenly snapped Billy back into reality.

"Maleficent," Billy asked, "are you talking to me? I'm sorry, but Tony and Andy didn't give me their itinerary. I have no idea how they got to his parents' new house. I know you say you don't give a damn, but one more word out of you about my friends, and I will be forced to tell all your new little minions the story of how the four of us came to have our gay little names for each other."

"Oh, my, my Billy, you old chicken hawk, you. You are way too upset this morning. What's got you so pissy on this bright and sunny morning?"

"I don't know, maybe it's that I have to go slumming, you know, sharing a dressing room with the likes of you."

Because the renovations on the principles' dressing rooms were taking so long, they found they had to dress with the male ensemble. Billy then went on to remind Donald he was not the only chicken hawk in the company.

"You're still upset Tony wouldn't give you the time of day, and he chooses to be with a dancer who actually has talent!"

"Billy, Billy, Billy, sticks and stones may break my bones, but the words from an old fagot like you, only make me laugh all the more!"

Billy was always more than willing to tell anyone who would listen, what truly happened the night 'the four fairies' got their nicknames. Donald, Andy, Tony and Billy had all worked together in a show over at the Winter Garden several years ago. Although Billy wasn't meant to be a part of it, he was unfortunately just another victim.

The incident started on closing night, and continued at the wrap party. They became known as The Four Fairies when a homophobic housekeeper, in the apartment where the party was held, returned to her bedroom.

She screamed in broken English. "Come help and stop them, 'The Fairies Men,' are going to be killing each other!"

Donald was twenty-seven years old, and Tony was only seventeen. Tony truly was beautiful, but young and dumb. When Donald and Andy met several years earlier it was lust at first sight, however, it was short lived. According to Billy, Andy had become smitten with the young, charismatic star. He soon left Donald in the dust.

Tony was one of the friendliest actors around town, gentle and kind to everyone he met. This was a rare quality in actors, and even more so in the acting community of gay men. In retaliation, Donald made advances towards Tony. Tony not wanting to hurt anyone's feelings blushed and walked away. It was perceived as Tony throwing down of the gauntlet. Donald decided that he was going to enjoy a romp in the sack with the pretty boy, regardless of how Tony or Andy or anyone else might feel about it.

Moments before Tony's last scene, Donald slipped a mickey into an open bottle of champagne that Billy and Tony had been sharing all night. Tony was done on stage except his final curtain call. Billy was not so lucky; he still had to get through the 11 p.m. closing number. Billy started to succumb to the drugs, and the microphones unfortunately picked up on everything he was babbling.

If he said it once, he'd said it a dozen times, "Get out of the way, I'm late, I'm late, late for my scene!" From that day forward he was known as 'The White Rabbit' from Alice In Wonderland. People within the Broadway community would see him on the streets, and break into song, "I'm late, I'm late, for a very important date," then walk away laughing.

Although it soon became monotonous, what happened to Billy was insignificant, when compared to what happened effecting Donald and Tony. Tony, almost comatose, was forced onto a small bed, and into a very compromising position. He was moments away from becoming another victim of Donald's lustful nature. Andy heard someone's muffled pleas to stop, when he opened the door to the housekeeper's bedroom.

Embarrassed by the entire incident, Tony never pursued legal action, even with the assistant district attorney being a family member.

From that date forward, the four men had new nicknames. Billy's was a reference to his tardiness on stage, and contributed to his ever-increasing need to be early.

The other three had mixed reactions to their nicknames. Tony refused the name of 'Sleeping Beauty'. Andy had no clue who 'Merryweather' was, but someone explained that she helped save Sleeping Beauty's life. Donald accepted his nickname of Maleficent as if it was an honor. There was no denying who he was, is, and forever will be, the most evil of all the fairies, on "The Great White Way!"

#

There were those moments when Andy couldn't think about what it was like to be hidden in the closet. Tony on the other hand refused to be outed to his father and brother. Meanwhile, the two lovebirds started to succumb to the pressures of their differing opinions.

"Don't you even start your crap with me. I love you, but I will not put up with your bullshit Andy. Don't look at me like that; you know exactly what I mean. Maybe it's been too many years living in Siberia, but sometime you can be such a fucking bitch."

"Tony, Moscow, I was raised in Moscow."

"Moscow, Siberia, St Petersburg, I don't give a shit."

Two out of the four bedrooms in the house were empty, and that was a good thing. There was nothing for either Tony or Andy to throw at the other person. Unfortunately, the room they were occupying echoed, and very loudly at that.

"Andy, I know you don't give a rats ass if you ever saw your family again, but I do. I'll be damned if I'll go without a nice visit with my baby brother. So, don't you even try and guilt me into anything. You know if the shoe was on the other foot and we were in Washington D.C. and you wanted some time with a sibling, I'd be taking a tour of 'The National Mall'."

Before Andy had the chance to respond, Tony stepped next door to Nic's room and knocked.

"It's open, come on in." answered Nic.

"Wow kid, your room looks nice! Grab your money, and let's get going." Tony shouted.

"What do you mean, grab your money, you invited me."

"Yeah, but with your brains, I thought you would have some extra money to take you charming older brother out!"

"You thought all that on your own, did you? You know what mom says; when it comes to money I am a true Mancini. She says I can starch a dollar till it screams bloody murder. I don't let a penny out of my sight. If you want me to advise you on a money management program, I'd love to help you."

"Man, it'd be easier to get blood out of a turnip, than money out of you."

After Tony found the payphone his mother told him about earlier, he called for a cab. Soon enough they found themselves at a local hot dog stand. If they had known about its location they could have walked there in no time. Tony thought just how wonderful it was being able to corrupt his baby brother with a non-kosher meal on a Sabbath afternoon. As the two walked in, all they could smell were the onions on the grill along with the French fries cooking in the deep fryer. The décor was lost on Nic, but Tony noticed all the 1930s and '40s ads suggesting they should enjoy a Coca Cola.

The Mancini brothers could always find something lighthearted to talk about, today however they questioned each other about what they thought was going on in the minds of both their parents.

Nic soon reminded Tony he was privy to having mom's ear through his weekly phone calls. Nic wanted to ask his older brother if he had any idea how crazy she would get on a Monday afternoon? He eventually confessed as to how crazy she could get on Mondays.

"Tony I swear to God, the house could be on fire and she didn't care, as long as she spoke to you. Come on Tony, you talk to her for hours on end, and she hasn't told you anything?"

"Well I could say the same thing of you. You and dad talk all the time. Do you think this radio thing is his mid life crises or what? Also, what does he think about how mom's been acting?"

Just about that time the lady behind the counter called out their order number. Nic started to joke about the non-kosher hotdogs, when the cashier assured them it was okay, that everything in the place was kosher. She told them that outside of Israel and New York, Ghent was the most Jewish place on earth.

"Tony, think about what you just said. Do you think for one second I talk to dad any more than I have to?"

"Are we crazy, I would kill to get dad to talk to me without a gin and tonic, and you want nothing to do with him."

"You know, we could always trade places. Forget I said that!"

"Why, what is so bad about my life?"

"Nothing I guess, but living with aunt Maria; she creeps me out."

"Really, she creeps you out does she? I thought you were going to say something about my job or my roommate."

"Tony, your roommate? Come on, I'm not that naive. Tony let's get real, both of us have our abnormalities."

"Abnormalities, what the hell are you trying to say Nic?"

"Well, come on some days I have the brain of a forty year old, while stuck in the body of a fourteen year old boy."

"Not sure if I should even ask, but what's my abnormality."

"Nobody, and I mean nobody can have that nice of a voice, come on you even snore harmoniously, and then there's your work. I mean come on already, how many people set their sights on something and go out and achieve it? Then, there is the fact that you're getting it on with another boy. I mean look at me, I like girls, or I think I do. Who knows maybe it's just their tits. I see a set and my mind goes crazy and my dick well, you know."

"When the hell did you become so, normal?"

"Can I get you to tell dad just how normal I am?"

"I don't think he would call me a good judge on what's normal or not."

It was just a second or two later that the ever so normal Nic, who had the social graces of a 14 year old boy, belched and passed gas louder than Tony thought was humanly possible.

"You know some people find that to be disgusting, me included! As a matter of fact I will be leaving now. I'm starting to question if you are the one I should talk to, after all."

"The one, the one for what?"

"Oh Nicky, I don't know."

"Tony don't you start that 'oh Nicky' shit with me, I still have that old man brain."

Yes, it's true that some brothers may have very little to do with one another. That was not the case with the Mancini boys, even after seven years apart from one another, never had two brothers been any closer.

"Nic how the hell do I do this? Shit, It's just, oh fuck, I don't know how to do this."

"Do what? Tony, you're starting to scare me, what's going on?"

It was with tears streaming down his face, he found the courage to tell his baby brother everything that was about to happen to him. He went on to tell his baby brother how much he hated placing such a burden on his shoulders. Yet he felt he had no one else to turn to. He begged Nic to try to step up to the plate and become the shoulder that he knew she was going to need. Tony went on to tell Nic that the day was coming where mom will be at the end of her rope. Then tearfully, he asked that when it happened he would just whisper in her ear, that Tony loves her.

"Please, Nic do that much for me, please."

"Tony Mancini, what the hell are you talking about?"

"In about twelve hours or so, I'll be dead."

"What."

"Okay, not the 'swimming with the fishes' dead. I mean, I'll still be alive, but no one will know me where I'm going. As of 2:30 am tomorrow Sunday July 31, 1971, Mr. Antonio Lorenzo Reuben Mancini aka Mr. Tony Mann, Broadway star, will have his lights dimmed once and for all.

# # #

"Hello, you good looking, sexy, strapping young specimen of hot, pure and raw manhood!"

"My God, you've been reading my mother's silly romance novels, haven't you?"

"Well I had to do something to pass the time. It was that or look at your dad's *Playboy* magazines."

"You chose wisely, my friend."

"So, my dear, how was your lunch with your baby brother?"

"It was very informative; my brother is a tit man. No it was good, but not as good as dinner with you is going to be!"

"Cool, I heard there's an Italian restaurant right down the street that we can walk to. How about pizza? If not, what about pasta?"

"Andy, pizza? Come on, never do on vacation what you can do at home. I've got something better in mind. Why don't we go get some surf 'n' turf?"

"Tony, you know we can't afford it?"

"We're not in the city, and stop being such a penny pincher. I say you go and wedge your skinny ass into your tightest blue jeans and put on that bright pink polo shirt I like. Then were off to go get a hotel room."

"But I thought we were going to the club tonight?"

"Andy, we are, but unless you want to make out in absolute silence, we need to go and get a room. Remember my brother is right next door. You'll have more opportunities to have your way with your, how did you phrase it again? Your sexy, good looking, strapping young specimen of hot, pure and raw lover!"

Leaving a note for his mother. Tony kept it very short,

Don't wait up for me; I'll be back as soon as I can.

The guys walked to the end of the block, and were lucky enough to hail a cab with in just a few minutes.

"Hey, I know youse two. I picked you up at the airport yesterday. Are you guys on your way back to the airport?"

"Not yet, but we want to go back to that hotel."

The cabbie grabbed the handle on the fare meter turning it clockwise by half a turn, and then put the car into drive. Tony discreetly slid his left hand across the seat and grabbed Andy's right one, and squeezed it.

Andy, usually the more observant of the two, seemed totally oblivious to Tony's emotional state. As he sat there he did his best to take in every curve and line of the face of the only man Tony had ever loved.

He also thought about the irony of what today was on the Jewish calendar. Although most Jews had long forgotten about it, at sunset Tisha B'Av would begin. Had his grandmother not taught him, he also would have had no clue as to its significance.

It would seem that the worst calamities happened that day. As odd as it was, both temples in Israel were destroyed on Tisha B'Av. Tony's world and everything in it were just a few hours away from also being destroyed. That was the real price for being in the wrong place at the wrong time.

"Hey Tony, you doing okay?"

"Yea, just a bit hungry, why do you ask?"

"Its just that you seem a million miles away."

"Sorry, it's just the most relaxing cab ride I had in years."

"You in a hurry to get back to the noise of Manhattan?"

Tony just shook his head, smiled and giggled a bit, then drifted back into his thoughts. His memories continued to circle around that afternoon when instead of strolling out onto center stage as any normal performer would to do their vocal warm up exercises. He was crazy and had gone to the front row of the balcony and sing down to the stage. He had been taught somewhere along the way, that from the highest point in the theater you could hear your weakest notes. Then you could work on fixing them. Who knew the city's most notorious extortionists, the theater manager and two of the show's producers, were using the show and theater as a means to launder money and distribute cocaine. They were hiding in the mezzanine, planning their next drug trafficking operation. He had hoped beyond hope that no one had looked up while he was running his vocal scales. Then for no more than a split second, his show producer caught Tony gazing down on them.

"Tony, hey Tony, you getting out of the cab? I'm sure this guy wants to move on, you know, make a living. As your mom said, not everyone's on a vacation."

"Oh, sorry about that mister."

As they walked into the hotel's lobby, the desk clerk recognized them and welcomed them back.

"Mr. Mancini, back so soon? Will the rest of your family be staying with us this evening?"

"No, not tonight."

"Will that be two single rooms?"

"No a double will do just fine. By the way, do you still have any tables upstairs available for dinner?"

"Mr. Mancini, I think we do, give me just a second. Let me see. We do have several duce tops open tonight; shall I hold one for you? Oh my, but I'm so sorry, tonight's special is not kosher, it's surf 'n turf. It's our regular special on Saturday nights, especially in the summer time. Then there's the fact, we're on the Chesapeake Bay. What could be better than that? Okay Mr. Mancini, that's a table for two at 8 p.m., perfect time to catch the setting sun! Mr. Mancini and guest, in the same room as last night."

The clerk tapped the porter's bell.

"Robert, help the... you're not Robert."

"Ya, I'm Peter, I'm just filling in for him tonight."

"Okay, please help these gentlemen with their bags."

"There are no bags, just us, so there's no need..."

"Mr. Mann, it would be a privilege to at least walk you to your door, you know, show you your room and all. Mr. Mann, Mr. Maxim, please forgive me for bothering you two. I know you guys are vacationing, but I just wanted to tell you that I saw you on stage about a month ago! Well, my roommate and I did. We just loved the show so much, please don't think I'm a crazed fan, and please don't tell my boss I asked, but I brought my playbill in hopes of seeing you two again tonight. Is there any way I can get you two to autograph it for me and James?"

Andy was about to knock Tony down in order to sign the playbill, then wasted no time in becoming the best of friends with Peter. Tony just stood there as if he had been drugged, or was having an out of body experience.

"Peter, it was so nice to talk with you, hope to see you later and maybe meet James."

"Peter and James, who are they?" asked Tony.

"Are you feeling okay?"

"I will be once were in the room, naked and I have me some, 'Afternoon Delight'!"

All the while, the noose which had been placed around Tony's neck on Friday morning as they departed LaGuardia was now starting to tighten ever so slowly. In addition, Tony almost tipped his hand when his gentle lovemaking turned ever so lascivious.

"Tony, have you lost your mind, what do you mean let's do it again?"

"I think it's all this heat and humidity, I've become a wild man!"

After a cool shower, both men took a nice slow walk up to the restaurant. However, there seemed to be a much more party like mood floating through out the dinning room.

"What's going on tonight, it seems a lot more lively." Tony asked of the waitress.

"What, were you here last night, with all the Bubbe and Zadie, oh I'm sorry that means..."

"We know, we know, in other words it was because of the Sabbath."

"You got it, oh do you two need a kosher meal tonight?"

"No that won't be necessary, how about a nice bottle of Pol Roger along with the special of the evening, cooked medium well, and a house salad served with a buttermilk dressing please."

"Yes, sir, right away, sir, however, I cannot bring you..."

"I forgot, the Commonwealth of Virginia and all its rules, bring us whatever you can, and thank you."

After they both had enjoyed a wonderful meal together, the guys again walked back to the room. No sooner had the hotel room's door shut, Tony striped naked and begged the ever so passive Andy to physically dominate him. Before the hour was up, Andy had given Tony everything he had to give, then asked Tony to do the same. After a dip in the swimming pool, then a hot shower, the men found their way to one of the local gay bars.

As both Tony and Andy walked towards the front door of the club, they noticed it had no signage or windows in front. As the door opened, two very large, physically fit men were standing side by side just a few feet inside the door. They had one purpose and that was to scare the bejesus out of any potential troublemakers. Behind what appeared to be a glass cage, sat an older, rather effeminate man who was collecting the cover charge. As the man returned the change to Andy's hand he held onto it just a second or two longer than either Tony or Andy would have liked. However, before the Ogres were willing to step aside, the troll behind the front desk had a question. One he insisted must be answered before the guys could gain access.

"Excuse me you two, but you must let me know what kind of bar this is!"

Tony grinned, grabbed Andy, and laid a lip lock on him for all the ages. The two bodybuilders broke out in laughter while applauding.

"Fabulous darlings, simply fabulous!" added the older gentleman. "Also, if for any reason the lights come on before the deejay calls for last call, stop dancing. It means that the Commonwealth has sent Vicky Vice to come in and harass all us little ole' queers. From that point on, it's every man or queen for themselves!"

As they walked between the two gentlemen, and into the inner sanctum of the club, Peter walked up. He appeared to be dragging another man with him, and then he proudly introduced his boyfriend James to both Andy and Tony.

As Peter grabbed Tony, he led him by the arm away from the other two men, and told him they just had to get through the next few hours. He reminded Tony that this protection agency may be new, but it works. Tony simply smiled and reassured James that he was committed to this. Also, that he and his associate needed to back off and allow him his last few hours to be spent with Andy.

"Mr. Mann, please let Pete and me get you the first round of drinks ... you know, southern hospitality and all."

"Well James, I am sure Mr. Mann and Mr. Maxim have drinks bought for them all the time."

"Peter, that is simply rude! Tony, Andy please forgive his lack of manners. I think it's best if we find our way to another bar for the night. Imagine if your boyfriend met one of his idols, then got to party with them. I can understand why he's a bit pissy. It was nice to have met both of you. "

Shortly after Peter and James exited the bar, one of the clubs waiters walked up to the Broadway stars, and asked if they were who he had been told they were.

"Hello, but are you Mr. Mann?"

"Maybe, why do you ask?"

"Peter and James wanted to buy you two a drink. Also they said they were sorry, but it was nice to have met you."

"Yes, but they just left, so how can they..."

"Don't worry, they took really good care of me. I was instructed to make sure you too had a load of fun tonight. So let's get started, what can I get you two gentlemen?"

" My friend here drinks Vodka."

"What kind?"

"He's Russian, and to him there is nothing but Smirnoff!"

"And for you sir?"

"I'll have a Shirley Temple."

"A what?"

"Its ginger ale and a splash of grenadine."

"Sir, with all due respect, I know what a Shirley Temple is. My question is why? You just look like you could handle the strongest of cocktails!"

"To tell ya the truth, Andy here enjoys drinking, and when he is happy, I'm happy."

"That is so sweet, but there has got to be more to it than just that. I'd love to know more."

"If I didn't know better, I'd think you are flirting with me."

"Sir, you would be correct, nothing ventured, nothing gained. Remember, I was told to make sure you enjoyed your evening."

"That sir is why I don't drink in public, I get into all kinds of trouble."

"Mr. Mann, I would love to get you into some trouble."

"I'm sure it would be a blast to be with you, I just know you could drive me crazy, but that man over there is my everything, so please stop."

"Wow, tall, dark, and devoted. Does he know how much you love him."?

"I do hope so."

As was often the case with Andy, he seemed to be a little uptight when outside his normal atmosphere, of home, the theater or in a bar environment. Then there were those last three shots of Smirnoff, which truly helped to loosen him up quite a bit. As Tony stood there, heart crumbling in his chest, he watched Andy enjoy the music and the movement of the crowd. All Tony could think about at that moment in time was that the only thing that brought him any joy was being with Andy, and of course, singing on stage! Both of which were about to disappear.

Andy ran to Tony and asked if they could come back tomorrow night as it seemed there was a drag show on Sunday night. Erica was the headliner and Andy knew it would be good for a laugh or two.

"Who is Erica?" Tony asked.

"He's our waiter, okay it's David, and the young man you have been talking to. Where have you been all night?"

"I've been right here watching you!"

Knowing how all this was going to play out, Tony quickly agreed to Andy's request for a return trip the following night. It was the deejay's announcement that reminded him that the witching hour was truly upon them.

"Ladies and gentlemen, boys and girls, children of all ages, you know what time it is don't you? It's your last chance for romance tonight, so grab that special someone and dance one more dance. By the way folks, the Russians are coming, the Russians are coming! This next song goes out to Andrei Maxim. It's Crosby, Stills, Nash and Young's 'Love the One You're With.' You all know I hate to say it, but, this is your last call, its last call, last call for alcohol."

Everyone moved to the dance floor, drinks in hand, only to have the entire wait staff try to confiscate the glasses. Moments later the deejay reminded everyone.

"You don't have to go home, but you can't stay here."

As the disco lights were all switched off, and the house lights rose, Tony knew it was time to sing his swan song. As the masses slowly began the migratory stampede towards the door, Tony and Andy had what was to become their last conversation.

"Hey cutie pie, do you want to go back to the room and try to sneak into the pool and go skinny dipping?" Andy asked.

"You really are messed up aren't you? I can tell you've had fun tonight! Go find us a cab, I'll meet you out there, I gotta go and piss something fierce."

Before walking away towards the restroom Tony reached over and pulled Andy's body close to his and gave him what he knew would be the last kiss they would ever share. Then he whispered into his ear,

"Ya lyublu tebya"

"Tony, I love you too, you okay? I'll see ya in the cab."

With his heart in his throat he turned away from Andy and walked into the restroom where he found two large men standing there, waiting for him. He managed to get a simple "Don't hurt him" out of his mouth as the tears began streaming down his cheeks, and then he dropped to the floor as he began to fall apart.

It was as a rather intoxicated Andy walked with a somewhat pronounced stagger out the door of the club, that two men who appeared to be federal agents approached him.

"Privet, moy droug!"

"Wow, your Russian is good, and hello to you, too."

Seconds later they took him by the arms and briskly helped him into a large nondescript step van. As the two men dragged Andy into the van, it's driver put it in gear and drove off.

"Mr. Petrov, please calm down, we need you to understand, this can end nicely, as in you can live to see another day. Or if you wish it could all go south."

As an actor, Andy knew better than anyone that in the real world, silence was golden yet backstage it was mandatory. For the next two hours, that's all there was. Eventually the van parked in front of a nice ranch styled home in a quite little suburban neighborhood.

"Mr. Petro, I want you to listen very carefully to me. I have two chooses for you, get out of this van and go knock on your daddy's front door or we continue on to New York City. With your history of defection, and your only real talent is dancing, it's not that hard of a decision. What will it be?"

"Yes, yes I'll go back to the city."

"You know Mr. Petrov, you must be doing something wrong, cause your karma is bad. Andy, may I call you Andy?"

Andy nods, not wanting to say or do anything wrong.

"Okay, Andy, this is what I would do. When you get back, don't go to your old apartment call a friend to stay with. Your boyfriend Tony is a wanted man, and if you want to live you will forget you ever knew him. Forget his name forget all about his family, as a matter of fact, never even say the name again. You should just keep your head down, your nose clean, and dance on the Great White Way as long as your body will let you."

# # #

"Tony, you know you've made the right choice, but now it's time to go out there and give your audience the big encore."

"Where have you all taken Andy?"

"There's all the time in the world for talking, after we get you in the van. We gotta get it in gear before someone walks in and blows our cover."

If ever there was a performance that should have earned a Tony award for acting, it was when the restroom door was pushed open so hard it could have come off its hinges. One of the agents picked Tony up by the belt as he hauled him to the door.

"Help! Help me please! They aren't real cops, please help me, none of this is real! Help me!"

"Mr. Esposito, you have the right to remain silent. Anything you say can and will be used against you in a court of law. You have a right to an attorney. If you cannot afford one, the Commonwealth of Virginia will appoint one for you. Do you understand your rights as I have read them to you?"

Just then one of the two men dragging Tony out the club's front door turned back to the bouncers and apologized for making such a scene. Before exiting he said, in a deliberately loud voice, "Law enforcement, it's not for the faint of heart!" One bouncer turned to the other and said, "Who would have known, they seemed to have fit right in."

The two federal marshals, who were better known to Tony as Peter and James, were asked if Andy knew anything yet?

"Let's see, he is in a van with three men he doesn't know. They are busy indoctrinating him with propaganda. The party line, persuading him that he doesn't know anyone named Tony, so on and so forth."

"As I told you the day I met you at your Aunt Maria's apartment over in Brooklyn, I am the only one you will deal with after we say good bye to James after our next stop.

Mr. Reuben Esposito, I want to remind you the person you were half an hour ago is now gone forever. Don't even think about whispering that name again."

With the passing of every hour, approximately a hundred miles or more came between both Tony and Andy. Although Tony was unsure of his final destination, he took solace in the fact that someone was there to help him through the transition.

FOUR

As much as Rico knew the primary reason he had been brought on board, he still felt somewhat like the new kid on the first day at a new school. He simply sat in the employees break room. He also did his best to eavesdrop on the two ladies at the other end of the lunch table.

"I'm sorry I didn't make it over to visit with you yesterday, God knows I love her, but you know how my mother is; she can be so draining sometimes. Tell me Cindy, how was your weekend? Did you get that lazy good-for-nothing husband of yours to take care of the lawn, or did you have to get the neighbor boy to do it for him yet again?" asked Kathy, from the accounting and payroll department.

"Kathy, you know I should just have you do a payroll deduction and send it directly to him. I'm so tired of begging Tom to do anything on a Saturday! He's forever telling me, he's gotta prepare for work tomorrow."

"Here's an idea, tell that old man of yours he'll never have to do the lawn work again. I'll just send William and the other church deacons over and let them do it for him."

"Yeah, can't you just hear the dish now? Pastor's wife "shames" her man into doing his own lawn work!"

"Cindy, think about what you just said, your husband, my pastor, he can't be "shamed" into anything! That man..."

"Forgive the interruption Kathy, but who is that dark haired gentleman sitting at the other end of the room?"

"He's the new man on campus. A Yankee, maybe a Damn Yankee, only time will tell."

"What's the difference?"

"I keep forgetting you really aren't a southerner, are you? A yankee is a person from up north who comes down south, but a damn yankee is the one who won't go back!

I'm sure after he meets you, he'll tuck tail and go running back up to that damned Big Apple."

"So we finally get to put a face to the personnel record, Mr. Enrico Lorenzo Mancini. WJDC's new messiah, I somehow thought he would be a bit taller. By the way, have you always disliked northerners?"

"Girl, are you crazy, you can't say stuff like that!"

"What, that I thought he would be taller. Or that you don't like people from up north?"

"No! You can't call him that, you know, messiah. Didn't you know he's Jewish?"

"You are kidding right? That's just what I'm hoping for; we need someone to become WJDC's much needed executioner, headhunter and yes messiah!"

Very few, if any of Rico's friends would have ever called him a messiah. He did, however, have the chutzpah to get the job done, at least the job that the radio station expected from him! They were looking for an executioner, as well as a headhunter and he fit the bill. He inherited his ability for those two tasks from his parents, Hannah Lynn and David Abram Mancini.

It was Hannah's humble opinion that David, her husband, and Rico's father had a beautiful face, a heart of gold, and also had the brain of a genius.

David Abram was valedictorian of their high school class, and was the first in his family to receive a college education.

They truly did complement each other; David and Hannah to the outside world appeared to be the perfect couple. Only a few friends knew the truth about their private lives. Those who knew them with the most intimacy would say that the Mancini's were anything but what they appeared to be.

Yenta should have been Hannah's middle name, as she truly was a busybody, busier than a body had the right to be! She was also a bit of a gossip, along with her love of being the proverbial "she-devil." After their marriage, which was prearranged. The proverbial smoke cleared and the deceitfulness rolled away, Hannah concluded that David was much less than the perfect man she had once envisioned him to be. He was not the first man to let his little ole schmuck do the thinking for him, as was the case with many a Mancini man.

Rico's parents had two children, both of whom had brains and nerve, but if they lacked anything, it was made up for with a bit of arrogance and a touch of brazen presumption.

Those traits served Rico's sister Sarah Maria Mancini well when she became the first female Assistant District Attorney in greater New York City. Maria was known for being fair, tolerant, and very strong willed. Much the same could be said of Rico.

"Mr. Mancini, it's nice to finally put a face with a name. My name is Cindy, not to be confused with Lucinda, one of our "on air" personalities. It will be my pleasure to help acclimate you to all the ups and downs, as well as the ins and outs, around here at WJDC."

Rico's first thought was about how small she was.

"Well, Miss, or is that Mrs. Cindy, I'm sure when it comes to looks, there will be no confusing the two of you!"

"That sir is an understatement, well never mind. You and I are heading across the street to The Recovery Room. It's the local hangout for the doctors and nurses, considering the hospital is only a block or two further west. It's the perfect place to keep our conversation just between the two of us. Also my husband the Reverend Thomas Webb Jr. would say its Mrs. Cindy Webb!"

Enrico took a step backwards, as well as one last glance at her backside, and thought, well that was a step in the wrong direction. He grabbed his faded old navy briefcase, and a moment later was double-timing it. She was giving him that look that suggested it would be best if he not keep her waiting. As he followed her, he started to think she could very well be one for suffering from a case of Napoleon Syndrome!

"Grab yourself something to drink, a soda or whatever, but no alcohol at least not on the company's dime, or on my time. I know you thought you were going to work for Thomas Webb, and you do. I just want you to understand what all is coming down the pike. The next few facts are going to blow your mind. First off you didn't come to us by chance. If you grow to love this job, you have two people to say thanks to. The first would be your old buddy Paco the Taco. You remember the taco eating champion from Texas. "

"Yea, Mrs. Webb, my wife Delilah and I were just up there for Cinco de Mayo. That's right, he said he knew of someone looking for a management type who might want to get into radio.

It had to be Paco who told Mr. Webb about my time working with the American Forces Korea Network.

That's where I fell in love with broadcasting. But how did you know about his taco eating history?"

"No to tell you the truth, it was my dad who told me about Paco. And he also told him about you, the crazy young man from Brooklyn who was a genius and loved radio."

"I'm sorry, but you have me at a disadvantage. Who is your dad, and how does he know me?"

"Mr. Mancini, go back about twelve years ago. You and Paco worked in the same office, right."

"Yeah, that was when we were stationed at Pearl Harbor."

"Oh my goodness, that's where I knew Mr. Webb from. All through the interview I kept thinking I knew this fellow, but he never said anything so nether did I. Wow, it really is a small world. But what does that have to do with your dad? I mean Paco told your father in law about me a few months ago, right?"

"Okay here it is, I'm 24 now, that was back when I was 12. I know I've changed, but really."

"My maiden name is Parkerson, Cindy Parkerson. Think about it for a few seconds..."

"Oh my Lord, you can't be that Cindy, little Cindy Parkerson! The Admiral's Cindy?"

"Yes, I told you I was going to blow your mind."

"How the hell is that old son of a bitch? Oh my I'm sorry, how's the old salty dog?"

"The old salty dog is doing just fine, or he will be once he gets back to playing golf again, and that's where you come in!"

"Now, Mrs. Webb, I'm sure I'm not going to be of any help to your father as far as his golf game goes, I'm not meant to be anybody's golf partner!"

"That's funny, but let me try to explain. The problem is my dad waits for his best friend, and golf partner, to return to the game. It's only after rescuing WJDC that this will be accomplished. This conversation is the only reason why you and I are sitting in a bar on a Monday morning. Admiral Parkerson, my dad, your old boss, is best friends with Admiral Webb, who as you now know is now my father-in-law. I did tell you it would blow your mind, didn't I?"

"Wow, the luck of the Irish is shining down on me, and I'm Italian."

"Mr. Mancini, I believe luck is for the ill-prepared, but if anyone is lucky, I would have to say it was my father-in-law to have found you."

Mrs. Cindy Webb may have worked as the office manager, but that was nowhere close to where her heart was. Being the only child of an admiral, as well as being married to an admiral's only child, she knew everything there was to know about being the dutiful child. It was because of this mindset she walked away from helping her husband Tom Jr., in the growing of their new church. Her sacrifice was not only to help Thomas Sr. save WJDC, but also to save a place that provided employment for so many others.

#

"Enrico Lorenzo Mancini, what the hell did you say to our son on Friday night to make him and his friend leave us so soon?"

"Woman, what the hell are you talking about?"

"You ass, you know damn good and well what I'm talking about. You must have said something to make him leave us so early, yet again."

"Stay away, what, they haven't come back yet? DeeDee, I love ya, but what the hell are you babbling about. What did the note say?"

"It said for me not to wait up, and he would see me as soon as possible."

"Well, there you go; you know how he is. If it's anything other than him being on a stage, he may or may not get around to it. Besides that, they are on vacation. That boy of ours, hell he's never gonna do anything more than he has to. You would think he might help his mother unpack boxes. Maybe even take her out to lunch. But to tell ya the truth, I wouldn't hold my breath waiting on him."

"Okay, I hate to say it, you might be right, but at what point should I start to get worried?"

"Hell, DeeDee, self-preservation tells me not even think about answering that one. I love you, but when was the last time you stopped worrying?"

"Damn it, Rico take me to the airport!"

"Take you, take you; you want me to take you to the airport, now? What the hell is up with you? You wanna go to the airport, then go! But you will be the one to call your own damn taxicab."

"Rico, if there was a telephone available I wouldn't ask you for anything!"

"By the way DeeDee, what the hell is at the airport?"

"Damn it Rico, my boys are at the airport, on their way home."

"DeeDee, look at me. Those two so-called men are not your boys. Andy or whatever his real name is isn't our child. It pains me to say it, but Tony cut those apron strings a hell of a long time ago. I know your going to hate me when I say this but, birds of a feather flock together. What I mean to say is that my lesbian sister has somehow become Tony's surrogate mother. Whether you want to admit to it, or not!"

It was with his last statement Delilah slapped Enrico catching him completely off guard.

"What the hell is your problem? Woman, have you lost your ever loving mind? Is there something that you want to tell me about? I mean my God, what has turned you into this crazy woman?"

"Don't you sit there and talk trash about my son."

"Woman, I know you won't believe it, but I love that boy. Come on already, it's not the end of the world. Hell, I've known the fact that Tony has sugar in his shorts for about ten years now. Hell, with my sister, it wouldn't take much to figure that one out. I also knew he wanted to grow up to be the next Peter Pan on Ole Broadway, and the ballerina from Belarus, is in fact his long time boyfriend.

I am so sorry if I said anything that made you think I don't love my crazy ass boy. Hell woman, I couldn't be more proud of our boy. He is a chip off the old block."

"Rico love ya, but you'll need to explain that one to me."

"Come on, I made it to the top in the Navy. I retired as a Master Chief."

"Yeah, go on."

"Is our son working in what do they call it Small Theater."

"I think you're thinking of Little Theater."

"Yeah and last year, did he not get himself a nomination for one of those Tony Awards."

"Rico, you mean to say, you knew all this, and still had pride in your son, and you never said a word about it?"

"Hell woman, I know lots of shit, doesn't mean I'm gonna run around yelling it from the rooftops. Those two men have got more chutzpah than most. They chose to live in Manhattan, that rat-infested hellhole. It's the dirtiest, highest, crime-ridden city in all of America. Well hell, Harlem and the Bronx have nothing on Manhattan. You know what they say about us New Yorkers, if we can make it there, we can make it anywhere. Those boys are gonna be just fine."

"But that's not like him at all. My Tony, he calls me every Monday morning."

"DeeDee, we will leave Nic here to deal with the phone company, and you and I can go up the street and call Maria's office, and find out if the boys came home early or something."

"Rico, I just know something's not right!"

As the morning became evening, several things were accomplished that day. Ma Bell showed up to install two wall phones, one for the kitchen and the other in the upstairs hallway. He was able to make contact with his sister Maria. When he asked her if she knew anything about Tony or Andy's whereabouts, he felt it like a knife being twisted in his gut. His sister wasn't just passing the buck; she was out and out lying to him. He knew not to push her anymore, as she was more than ready to fall on her own sword.

"Delilah, my sister says she hasn't heard a thing from the guys. I don't want to be a naysayer, but since they arrived here on an earlier flight, you know they could have departed earlier. If you feel the need, we can go out there to see if they got on that flight. Do you know the flight time or number?"

"I remember Andy saying Tony said it was the last flight out to New York, I think it was at 9:15 p.m., just before the closing of the airport."

Rico and Delilah called a cab and went to the Norfolk airfield by themselves. They reminded Nic to be in bed before the local news broadcast began, and they'd be home as soon as possible.

"I'm so sorry ma'am, but this counter is closed already, Potomac Air, to your left, has the last incoming flight for the night."

"No, you don't understand, I am here to see my son off to New York."

"Well ma'am, then I am truly sorry, that flight left almost an hour ago."

"No, it doesn't leave till 9:15 p.m."

"On Friday and Saturday nights maybe, but Sunday through Thursday it's at 7:40 p.m."

"Are you sure?"

"Ma'am, with all due respect, I've been closing this counter down for almost a year now."

It was only after Delilah described Tony and Andy in great detail, that the representative said she had seen both men together, however, it was last Friday as she was just starting her workday.

She remembered looking at them both thinking, fashion-wise, the big city has finally come to the small town. She apologized to Rico and Delilah for not being able to be any more assistance, and then quickly disappeared from behind the counter.

#

"Hello, gorgeous, and welcome to Shear Delights."

"Good morning, Stella, is Annie in this morning?"

"Yes ma'am ah, but you need to have an appointment."

"I'm not looking to receive a service, today, just an ear to bend. I was here on Saturday morning for my first visit, and just felt so at ease with Annie."

"At ease, with Annie, yeah you and everyone else in town! You say your first visit was last Saturday morning, two days ago Saturday morning?"

"Well it was more like early afternoon."

"Oh, I feel better now. I pride myself on not forgetting a face or a name. Last Saturday afternoon, I started the happy hour just a bit early. For a moment I didn't recall you at all. Let me see if I can find her."

Before Stella had even begun to leave the reception desk, Annie came walking through and looked at her newest client.

"Hi Delilah, how was your hubby's first day at the new job yesterday?"

"Oh my goodness, I can't believe it, I forgot to ask him!"

"My, my, if it wasn't for being married for, what did you say, twenty years, I'd say you must be new at this wife game! Just remind him about the 'little bundle of joy.'

That alone should get you out of the dog house for the next several months."

"Annie, how on earth did you know about the baby? I haven't told anyone."

"I'm part bloodhound don't ya know. I must have smelled the little one on ya silly girl, ask anyone around town and they'll tell ya, I just know this stuff before it happens. Are you a Jap or a Goombah?"

"Annie, I'm sorry, but what are you asking me?"

"How the hell did you ever make it out of Flatbush? I'm asking you if you want to break bread, share some wine with me. You know as a Jap, a Jewish American Princess, you can't do nothing cause it might not be kosher.

Or are you a Goombah, you know, a godfather, a close friend. Make that a very close friend. In other words, is it L'chaim or Salute?"

"I knew I was gonna like ya the moment I met ya! Salute, and pass the wine!"

The two ladies found their way into the back room, where they shared a sleeve of saltines and half a carafe of wine. In addition to Annie sharing an apology for Stella's words on Saturday afternoon, they also shared a good bit of their life stories. Turns out Annie, more so than anybody else, could understand where Delilah's head and heart were at this moment in time. She had lost both, her husband and only child, a son, in a subway crash in midtown Manhattan in the spring of 1962.

As much as Stella, Margaret, and Beatrice, had been working long before the crack of dawn. It was with the clock striking nine that more of Annie's employees made their way into the shop. Some of them with a spring in their step, others were dragging themselves to their beauty stations. As if compelled to be fashionably late, Kenny flung open the front door, and announced to all that he had arrived.

"Hello darling, my name is Kenny, and thank the Lord above I'm the only rooster in this little ole' hen house. You know with me being one of the busiest operators here, you and I are going to be inseparable."

"Well Kenny, I must say it's nice to meet you, but why are we going to become so close?"

"You are the new shampoo girl, aren't you?"

"No Kenny, I am sorry to disappoint you, but I'm one of Annie's new clients."

Annie stepped between them and thanked Kenny for stepping up and folding some of the shampoo towels. Kenny gave her a look that simply said he wasn't following. Again Annie thanked him for going and finding some towels to fold, and then she gently led Delilah to the door. Annie reminded Delilah of her appointment on Friday afternoon, and before closing the door, told her that fixing hair was only part of being a beautician, and if she was needed for any reason, simply call her.

After a nice walk home Delilah admitting to herself she had lived long enough to have learned you get more flies with honey than with vinegar. So when she called her sister-in-law's office once more, she told herself to keep a civil tongue in her head.

She tried her best to get any new information of the whereabouts of Tony or Andy. She had to bite her lip when Marie gave her the cold shoulder.

She later remembered one of the tricks Tony had taught her on how to get information from the box office. You call with a hint of impropriety in your voice, and they would spill the beans, hopefully. She implied that she was with the *Village Voice* and was wondering if they had a response to the rumors going around that the producers had let Mr. Tony Mann go from the show.

Just a moment later she went out on a limb, and decided to make something up. She asked if Mr. Mann's termination was the reason for all the problems at the box office last night. Delilah knew at worst they would hang up on her, however at best she might get some kind of new information.

What Delilah heard next gave her no comfort, but at least it was something new.

"Ma'am, as the house manager said last night, Mr. Mancini was scheduled for a week's vacation, and there was a simple mix up. For the next two week, Mr. Mancini's understudy will be filling in. If you want a full refund, please feel free to come by the box office during normal business hours."

# # #

Never having been so scared after coming to the United States, Andy was a bundle of raw nerves the afternoon he visited with his long time agent.

"Ackerman and Ackerman Talent Management, how may I direct your call?"

If Andy had heard those words once, he had heard them a thousand times while waiting for his agent Joseph to walk out of his office and into the lobby. Most of Joe's greetings began with a hardy handshake, and a loud and robust, 'How's it going kid?', but not today. Just as the office door began to close, the receptionist attempted to enter behind Andy. He was so startled he jumped and caused her to drop the tray with the refreshments on it.

"Andy, it's not a problem at all. By the way, your appearance really has changed, hasn't it?"

"Joe it's funny, but the few friends I've seen say I look better with all the hair gone. Who knew shaving the head was so difficult. If I grow the hair back out I might dye it dark brown. I do know I'll never let the red grow back! Lord only knows how long I will need to keep this espionage lifestyle."

"Come on Andy, tell me already, what the hell happened? Did anything happen or change with Tony leading up to this?"

"Out of the blue! I swear one night Tony and I we're partying in the club after a show. The next thing I know, he didn't want to go out to any of the clubs. Hell, I'm the dancer; and if I pulled a hamstring and wanted to go home to rest, he would say I was the party pooper. Joe, what do I do?"

"Do you think he was kidnapped?"

"Again, I don't know what to think. I was told it would be best for me if I went back to New York. Keep my head down and my nose clean. This had nothing to do with me! And if I ever said his name out loud, it would as if I was killing all of his family!"

"My God, you truly are a better man than I am. I would have had a heart attack."

"They told me to never say anything. All I know is that I will never be able to say his name out loud again. The guy in the van put the fear of God in me! Again, I don't know what the hell happened."

But I didn't come here to bore you with all this crap! I need work, hell; I'll do drag and audition over at Radio City as a Rockette. You think anyone would hire me?"

"Come on Andy, they won't let you return over at 'JC Superstar'? Come on, all you need is a fake beard and a wig."

"Joseph, think about what you just said. You want that I should go back, knowing Donald and all his little demons are just waiting to chew me a new asshole, then spit me out? Also, the men in the black trench coats told me to lay low for as long as possible."

"Andy, I know this will sound like the kiss of death, but you know you are under contract with Jesus Christ Superstar. You know I'm in your corner. I can put in a call to some friends. Let me put my ear to the ground and see what I can do. I know someone starting a workshop about a bunch of dancers and the audition process. Andy I can't imagine the hell you've been through. Go get fitted for a dark brown wig and I'll talk to you later.

FIVE

Ever since Adam bit into Eve's apple thousands of years ago, men have been looking for a way to fix what ever the proverbial problem might be. That's why after they returned home from their first service at the new temple; Delilah was shocked that Rico continued calling his sister. He called her rather late on a Friday night, simply because he hoped after her having four or five glasses of wine she might be a little more loose lipped. Delilah and Rico hoped to hear something new from her, although he doubted he would. It would seem as if Maria's stonewalling could continue forever.

Trying her best to remain hopeful she found herself questioning the possibility of such a place as Purgatory existing. If it did, was it just for the dead? At times she felt they might have found themselves in the midst of it. Had this quaint little town become a holding place in their lives? Were they on their way down the path to hell itself, or might heaven be right around the next corner?

Rico was slowly growing colder, withdrawn and sullen. She had also changed due to Tony's disappearance; she found herself being more self-centered and hard-hearted. Were David Mancini, Rico's father's words starting to become a true prophecy?

What Delilah's father-in-law said to her, before their first anniversary, continued to haunt her! He came to her while Rico was still in Korea, and told her that the sins of the father were often passed onto the third and fourth generations. He explained with little if any emotion that both he and his father had cheated on their wives. He also told her she should not be surprised when, or if, she found out that Rico had followed on the same path.

Had Rico shut himself off from his family? Had he sought out an emotional refuge elsewhere, or were Delilah's hormones and the loss of her first born, starting to close in on her? It was seven weeks to the day that Tony had gone missing, and it was also Erev Rosh Hashanah, when Rico's facade started to show cracks, along with signs of a possible collapse!

"I'm sorry babe, I didn't mean to wake you again."

"Rico, I can't wait 'till tomorrow morning when you can stay home and sleep in a bit. Also, don't forget that if you can't get home tonight by five o'clock, please call me and I will rush down to the station and bring you one of your suits. From there we can go directly to the synagogue. After the last three years if you make me miss the shofar blowing, you won't have to worry about making amends with me, God, or anyone else, because I'll kill ya myself."

"Babe, I got to work tomorrow morning; in the real world it's just another workday. Remember, if I don't work, we don't get paid."

"You mean to tell me you've been there seven weeks, and you can't take the High Holy Days off work?"

"What, did I stutter? I swear you only hear what you want to hear. I told you several weeks ago about the drug bust at the radio station. The fact is we are down three deejays. Advertisers are abandoning ship, and I've got to maintain the status quo. We've got a kid on the way, and that rocket scientist son of ours will probably be ready for college next week, so no, I can't take tomorrow off work!"

"Rico, you're the manager. You can take the day off. It won't be the end of the world if you do!"

"Babe, I'm a civilian now. I jump through someone else's hoops. Before I was one among thousands, the days of putting in a chit and hoping for the best are gone forever. I am now the one who can be replaced in a heartbeat. I'll be damned if I'll move back home and start bussing tables with your mom as my boss, while she looks down her nose at me."

"Please."

"Damn it Delilah, enough! Would you just shut up about it already! I'll go tonight, then again in another ten days, but other than that, no more Temple 'till Passover. Enough with the religious crap already! Got it?"

"I'm sorry Rico, please forgive me for nagging at you."

"Just let it go, DeeDee, you didn't do anything."

As soon as Rico got dressed and hit the bottom step, Nic met him.

"Dad, give me a ride to school!"

"Dad, give me, give me, give me. How's this, I'll give you a piece of advice. Get the fuck out of my way. I'm not in the mood."

"But Dad, it's raining out there."

"Damn it boy! What is it, five or six blocks? Put on your raincoat and walk your butt on down the street to school."

"Dad, I don't have a rain coat, we moved here from San Diego. Remember, southern California!"

As the Mancini men got into the car, Nic asked, "Why is Mom so witchy lately?"

"Nic, I think the word you're looking for is bitchy. It's okay to say it amongst other men, and I think it has everything to do with your sister!"

"How do you know the baby will be a girl?"

"I don't know why, it's just that I have a hunch. Because when your mother was pregnant with you two boys she was, well, a lot nicer."

"But she was also a lot younger back then."

"When the hell did you grow to know it all, know it all, know it, all?"

It was only seconds later that Nic noticed his father's eye starting to twitch, along with the side of his mouth drooping. It was as if he was looking at the half smile of the 'Mona Lisa', yet on his dad, it was not a good look.

"Dad, are you okay? You're acting a little strange. Dad you're starting to scare me! Dad!"

Who could have known that when Tony asked Nic to give support to his mother, it would be his father who would end up being the one who was truly in need of it, and the one who would fall apart. After watching the tears roll down his father's face and his upper lip begin to quiver, Nic thought it best if he found his mother. He got out of the car, ran into the house and dragged his mom out to the car to help his dad! She yelled at Rico a few times, then turned to Nic and told him to go and get the operator on the telephone, and have her send some help.

Nic also had the wherewithal to call his dad's employer and tell them that his dad was on his way to Norfolk General, and that he wouldn't be in this morning. As Delilah learned that day, men tend to survive heart attacks; yet, they rarely survive strokes.

It's when you took into consideration what day it was on the Jewish calendar, some might have said what happened next was somewhat miraculous. While the young man working the admissions desk asked dozens of questions, everything came to a screeching halt, when the simplest of questions was asked.

"Religion?"

"What, huh?"

"I'm sorry to have to ask all these questions, but what is his religion?"

As Delilah answered, the young man looked up at her and asked her, "Would you like to have a rabbi pray with you?"

"Young man, I am sure your heart is in the right place, but today, of all the days of the year, what is the likelihood of finding one here, today? You are more likely to find a pound of bacon in my kitchen, than find a rabbi in this hospital."

"Mrs. Mancini, I just want to let you know my rabbinic ordination is coming up in about three weeks. So today might just be the day for a miracle to happen, that is if you and your son want, I would be more than willing to pray a blessing over your family!"

It was after the young rabbi and Delilah had finished praying that Rico's doctor introduced himself to both Nic and Delilah. He explained to Delilah that she would do more good for her family from within the walls of the synagogue than from the hospital's waiting room.

She left the hospital, long enough to go over to the radio station, where she met up with the owner, Mr. Webb. She remembered having met him at the company's Labor Day picnic. She updated him on Rico's condition and prognosis, and she was pleased to report that both were surprisingly good.

Mr. Webb asked to be updated as often as possible, and assured Delilah that Rico was in no danger of losing anything at the station. They would automate the overnight timeslot and move the deejays around in order to fill in during Rico's absence. Mr. Webb told her to go and enjoy tonight's service, and to give Rico best wishes from his work family!

As Monday turned into Friday, the doctor gave Rico a clean bill of health, along with orders for a bland, wine-free meal, before his evening in the synagogue. He also told him to stay home from work for the remainder of the high holydays allowing himself time to enjoy Yom Kippur.

"Mr. Mancini, yes I am a doctor, but I'm also a person of faith. As I told your wife your lucky to still be with us. Enjoy the Sabbath, and try to make atonement with everyone you can!"

# # #

As Rico's recovery continued, early September became late November, and his memory of Tony, and even his own stroke, became faint memories. Other changes in his life included the changing of his on air name, as well as his relationship with Miss Lucinda Chue. While in the studio, it was WJDC's Ricky & Lucy in The Morning Show. However, while in a certain young lady's penthouse on the seventeenth floor, it was more like Adam & Eve, or Romeo & Juliet.

"Okay boys and girls, Ricky Mann here with ya, along with everyone's favorite, Miss Lucy Chue. I don't know what you all call that white stuff falling from the sky, but when I took this job I was told it rarely, if ever, snowed here. So what do you all call it?"

"Listen to us, Rico. You grew up in Brooklyn, and I grew up in Japan, and yet we are the ones whining the loudest!"

"It's a cold, wintery, white morning out there," Rico said on air. "I'm here on this bone-chilling, cold morning, and as I was saying I'm from Brooklyn's very own Flatbush, so growing up I used to walk around the city in stuff like this, it doesn't bother me at all.

The problem is you guys don't have enough taxicabs on a good day, much less today. By the way, it's on a day like this I really do miss the subway system."

"So Rico, I bet you also had to walk to school uphill both ways, with gale force winds in your face! What? Are we supposed to feel sorry for you? Lucy Chue here with you, and let me tell you, this guy doesn't know snow. Like I was saying, I grew up northwest of Tokyo, in what's known as the Japanese Alps. I know snow. You want to talk snow, call us and let us know the deepest snow you have ever seen."

"Rico, I can't believe it's only 29 days 'till Christmas and Saint Nick will be with us on the Granby Street Mall tomorrow morning from 9am till noon. Rod Stewart on the way, Maggie, I think he's got something to say to you. After that it's Joan Baez with 'The Night They Drove Old Dixie Down.' By the way, your 'Dock Side' time and weather is, 8:40 and here's some news for ya, it's snowing and will be all day long! On its way at the top of the hour, we've got some Three Dog Night with 'Joy to the World,' followed by Miss Janis Joplin's 'Me and My Bobby McGee'."

"Folks, before we play any more music, I just want to say, I truly missed getting to hang out with Lucy and all of you yesterday morning. Lucy I just want to say thanks for doing the show solo. I loved hanging out with my wife and son. I know everyone enjoyed my absence. All of us here at WJDC hope you had a perfect Thanksgiving Day. Since today is the first official shopping day of the Christmas season, Miss Lucy Chue will be on assignment later this morning over at the Granby Street Mall to talk your ear off, if you let her. Well, let's rethink that, if she can get over to the mall. Your WJDC time is 8:44 and if you need to impress the boss today, I hope you're already at your desk, otherwise you, my friend are, oh what's the word I'm looking for, oh yeah, you're late. All roads heading south are stop and go; Hampton Boulevard, Granby Street and Tidewater Drive are no better than parking lots with all the snow falling. If my cohort, the lovely Lucy, hadn't already headed out wherever it was she is going this morning, she would be at her microphone telling you about the weather right now. We all know what's going on, Old St. Nick is sending the snow in preparation of his arrival on the mall tomorrow morning. Who are we kidding? Everyone's getting ready for his arrival. My son is thrilled, or maybe it's just the snow, since we just moved here from San Diego, and before that we lived in Pearl Harbor, so he's new to this snow thing. Back with ya in just a few!"

As soon as the microphone was turned off, Rico removed his headphones, and a telephone receiver was sitting between his head and his shoulder. His first statement to Mrs. Cindy Webb was that she was not to worry about a thing!

"Lucy and I have everything under control, it's no big deal being here all day long, just the two of us! As long as we have power, we'll stay on the air."

"This just in, the Granby street mall is calling it quits for the day. Also, if anyone sees a Popsicle wearing headphones and carrying a microphone and answering to the name of Lucy, send her back to the station, we all miss her back here. Next up, we are going into the time vault, back to 1963. We got Smokey Robinson and The Miracles with... a subject no one around here would ever think of, 'Let it Snow'."

No sooner had Rico turned his mic off then he saw Lucinda come running across the parking lot. It took her no time to get into the station and pour both herself and Rico a piping hot cup of coffee.

"Lucy, I'm glad you managed to get one of the guys to drop you back here, on their way home. No pride here, I got no problem with you being the qualified sound engineer, knowing all about how the EBS works. Hell, I barely have the script memorized. "This is the Emergency Broadcasting Service."

"Silly boy, it's called a system."

"Oh, Emergency Broadcasting System, if this had been an actual emergency the broadcasters in your area... hell, I'm just the stations manager and a part time deejay. So where's that Saké you said you had? Is it in your locker or what? Did I tell you the first time I drank Saké I was only nineteen and in Korea."

"Has Cindy called in this morning?" asked Lucy.

"Yeah, I told her not to worry, we would be okay here all alone, and we would keep our audience entertained. I didn't tell her we planned to keep each other entertained for as long as we could.

I can't believe it, would you just look out there at one of the busiest streets in town, and it's a virtual ghost town. We could get naked and fool around in the studio's bay window and no one would be the wiser.

Hey do you think Cindy would figure it out if we played Dylan's 'Desolation Row,' what is it like eleven or twelve minutes long? That should give us time enough for a bit of a quickie."

SIX

As Nic Mancini's namesake, the Italian philosopher Niccolo Machiavelli once said, "The more sand that has escaped from the hourglass of our lives, the clearer we should be able to see through it."

The operative word there is "should," because Rico wasn't seeing anything clearly these days. He truly was 'going through life with blinders on,' and yes, it's tough to see.

"Mr. Mancini, Mama-san, I am so honored to have you grace my humble home with your presence tonight. May I take your coats for you? Mrs. Mancini, with this evening being Mr. Mancini's favorite night of the year, why isn't Nicky attending our little soiree?"

"Miss Chue, there are no soirees for our Nicky. He most emphatically stated he would be staying at home in order to watch Dick Clark and his new 'New Year's Eve Show' tonight. He, like his father, will not be talked into, or out of, anything once he sets his mind to it."

"Yes, Mrs. Mancini, your husband reminds me of my baby brother, in that manner."

It was only after Lucy walked away that Delilah turned to Rico and said, "So Rico, that's her, the one you spend all your on air time with? Funny, but on air, her voice somehow sounded so much more Americanized.

She lives in this penthouse here on the seventeenth floor. So, this is what today's young adults call 'a humble home.' Also, please correct me, but did I hear her refer to me as 'Mama-san?' Why did she call me 'Mama-san?'"

"DeeDee, I'm sure it was meant as a term of endearment."

"Calling it a term of endearment doesn't make it so! Somehow I'm sure it wasn't meant to be anything close to endearing. No, my dear, I am not that foolish, but then only another woman would see it for what it was. By the way, please let her know I have never been in a brothel, in Asia or elsewhere. I'm sure she'll understand!"

History has often shown that the middle child is a remarkable team player, regardless of their older siblings leadership. That evening, the guests of WJDC's black tie affair saw nothing in Delilah but the most joyful and charismatic team player, regardless of how she was feeling about the other players. It was her pure elegance and diplomacy, along with her adorable pregnancy waddle, that led the existing, and potential advertisers, to sing the praises of the radio station's new management.

It's funny how some people are drawn to one another, but after the Halloween and Christmas parties, Delilah found herself wanting to socialize with only a few, and they were Jim Dandy, his wife Elizabeth, and two of the interns from the station's staff.

After spending a bit of time with Liz, comparing notes on the who's who in the WJDC staff, Delilah got the feeling that Rico was up to no good. She excused herself and went on a hunting party.

What she found was not what she was expecting!

"Are you crazy?" Rico asked one of the younger staff members.

"Guy Lombardo on New Year's Eve, along with some simple jazz, is the standard in tradition."

"But Mr. Mancini, I thought we were trying to become more hip."

"We will one day, but we need to make those old men in there with all that old money, happy. You got it kid?"

Delilah appeared from around the corner. "Rico, leave that poor young man alone. He's trying to earn a living. Would you please go and find us another glass of wine?"

She smiled at the young man who was playing deejay for the evening's soiree. "He means well, your boss that is, but he's older than he thinks he is. I was just out on the balcony and couldn't help but see the lighted sign for the radio station on the other side of the apartment complex's parking lot.

Allow the jazz to continue playing. As cold as it is, I want you to run quickly over to the station and get the hottest tracks you can find, bring them back up here, and then when the New Year's countdown is over, play like you're sick and tired of being an intern, and get ready for a pay raise. You hear me young man?"

"Yes ma'am, Mrs. Mancini."

As the eleven o'clock hour began, the party grew, along with the swelling of the music. It transformed Delilah and Rico into Ginger Rogers and Fred Astaire, as they danced all night. For all the fun Delilah and Rico appeared to be having, both of them as many others might have done, they mentally revisited the highs and lows of the year. 1971 was a year of landing his dream job, buying his first house, and meeting his newest mistress. Delilah however had to say so long to many a good girlfriend back in California. She also said goodbye to any chance of becoming an empty nester anytime soon.

With Rico's love for New Year's Eve growing each passing minute, brought about this foreboding feeling that grew within his heart and mind. It was as if he was standing before the precipice, and his only thought was 'Auld Lang Syne', for the sake of old times!

# # #

Not even three weeks into the New Year and Rico found himself back in the hospital. This time, however, he was not the patient, but the husband of the patient. Delilah's water broke shortly after the third Shabbat Service of the New Year. If Delilah's previous labors were any indications, she would be in need of her three Ds; doctor, doula, and a delivery room, and all of them, would be needed rather quickly!

Rico was in Korea when Tony made his proverbial début during the musical "The King and I" in the lobby of the St. James Theater on West 44th Street. Somewhere between the songs, 'I Whistle a Happy Tune' and 'Getting To Know You,' Delilah's water broke. Before either the King or Anna could begin to sing one of the final songs, 'Shall We Dance,' Tony was ready for his first curtain call.

Nic, however, was in no real hurry to arrive. Delilah was able to have at least two out of the three things she wanted when he came along. She made it to the hospital, and luckily her best girlfriend at the time was her doula, or labor coach. Unfortunately, her chosen doctor was nowhere to be found. It turned out that the afternoon Nic showed up, the doctor was out of town for Memorial Day.

As Delilah's labor pains continued in intensity and duration, it was beyond anything she had ever experienced with Tony or Nic. She began to grow apprehensive. She cried out, asking for Liz, Jim Dandy's wife, who was a pediatric nurse and also her chosen doula. Annie's sister Betty had begged for the honor, yet, Delilah chose Liz for obvious reasons.

After almost twelve hours, and only dilating a few centimeters, her doctor ordered an epidural. This was to help Delilah deal with the pain, but to also help keep the little one from going into fetal distress. Within half an hour of the epidural being administered, the call was made to change tactics and start prepping for an emergency C-section.

# # #

It was on Friday, January 29, 1972 that the conservative Temple found itself opening its doors to a host of goyim, which included Betty, Annie, and their brother Thomas, the minister from the Lutheran Church across from Shear Delights. One might have thought that was the making of a powder keg. Adding to the mix was almost every employee from WJDC, along with several clients and many of the hairdressers from Shear Delights.

Included were people who had not seen the inside of a house of prayer for many years. Yet, that night, they were all there to show their love and support for the newest member of the Mancini Family.

As the Rabbi looked out over his congregation and saw the amount of goyim, the non-Jews, he chose to give a quick and fun version of Judaism 101. As he joked, he was sure most knew the differences between the boy and the girl ceremony. With the girl, it was simple, no cutting, no blood, and no screaming, at least not from the child. The parents and family, now that was a different story!

"We wrap the baby in a 'tallit,' the prayer shawl, and pray she will grow in health and goodness, and commit her life to doing many a good deed. Also, that someday she too will have a husband and children of her own."

"Keeping with the family and Jewish tradition the new arrival was given the following name. Mary, for all the Italians, Hadassah for the Hebrew, Susan for all the goyim in her life, and lastly the family's name. Mary Hadassah Susan Mancini."

Moments later, everyone who knew what to do were erupting in a most celebratory fashion as the Rabbi lifted Mary up towards the ceiling with shouts of Mazel Tov, and more shouts of 'L'chaim.'

#

Before walking into the overly crowded flower shop, Rico asked himself, why he was about to stand in a line, and shell out a ton of money?

He also thought that with his being Jewish, why would he celebrate the day a Roman Catholic Priest was killed? After all, it was only Saint Valentine's Day.

Then there was the fact that Lucy was a Buddhist. As he stood there and watched three more men walk in he knew why, it's just one of those silly things were expected to do. As he stood in the line just to get up to the counter, he found himself asking yet another thought provoking question. How did I come to sleep through my life? If he could have been able to hold a conversation with himself as a younger man, would he have done what he thought was the right thing to do at the time?

It was only after a night of wedded bliss, and several trips to the land of milk and honey; that Rico thought to himself, this is it? So, this is what all the boys who have made a pilgrimage to the Promised Land keep talking about? As Peggy Lee asked in her hit song, 'Is that all there is?' There has got to be more to sex than this. It has been said of men they all have their 'type;' unfortunately, for Rico and Delilah he didn't marry his. No, he married the girl next door, his high school sweetheart. Another unfortunate problem for the two of them was that it would require his traveling seven thousand miles to find out what his true type was.

Close to six months in country, and the company's newest Yeoman proved his worth. How do you pay back the enlisted man who just spotted a major mistake and kept several officers from getting short-changed on their next payday? That's easy. You welcome him into the officer's club, get him drunk, and set him up with one of the local prostitutes.

Rico made a whirlwind of a discovery; prostitutes may know how to drive a service man crazy, but there is a price to pay!

The Navy's Corpsman who treated Rico knew he was married. Being a virtuous man, and knowing Rico had a bride back state side; he made damn good and sure the shot hurt like hell. He chose the largest needle he could find to administer the antibiotics to cure his gonorrhea.

Rico found himself a husband at eighteen, a war veteran at nineteen, and a father at the age of twenty. He also found himself playing house and becoming one of the many American men who contributed to the growing cultural problem in Korea known as 'Amerasians'.

July of 1953 found many military men and women leaving South Korea, as the war had come to somewhat of a close. Rico was not one of those personnel. His duty assignment kept him there for several more months, allowing the U.S. government to close up shop.

It also allowed Rico time to say goodbye to both his second son, as well as the child's mother. The woman he would have given anything to stay with.

If ever there was an emotional conflict within a person's life, it was now, at least that's how Rico saw it. No matter how well protected he may have been, he had just finished three years of war. As odd as it seemed, Rico felt more freedom during this time in a war zone than he had ever felt growing up under the eye of his mother back stateside. With that firmly planted in his mind he thought about not only having to face her, but also his bride back state side.

The hardest part of returning to a post-war life would be leaving his son behind. The child who he knew would be shunned as nothing more than a half bread. He would also need to remove his mistress's name from his vocabulary. Then there was telling Delilah about what was going to become their next duty station. He knew, without a doubt, that he had changed since moving away from Brooklyn. How had she grown and changed, and was she going to go along with his desires?

It was at the age of twenty-one Rico knew where he wanted to live for the rest of his days, Pearl Harbor, on the island of Oahu. As much as these eight islands had seen their share of hell, there was talk of better days ahead, with statehood just around the corner.

Delilah felt almost jubilant about moving to the islands. Little did she know that she was probably leaving the frying pan and jumping into the fire. It was Rico who wanted to keep ownership of his cake and yet be allowed to eat it too. He wanted to continue serving his country in the southwest Pacific Rim. He thought if he couldn't be with the lovely little ladies of paradise, he could at least continue to dream about them on a daily basis. He didn't think there was anything wrong with asking for everything! After all, he just wanted his bride, his child and any lovely ladies he could find.

# # #

It can be said there is a world of difference between intelligence and wisdom. Wisdom tells you not to shit where you eat. Intelligence tells you your wife will never find out about the woman you brought home to her bed.

"I'm telling ya Lucy, that woman has never ever changed a thing, once it is set in motion, never, ever. She won't start packing till the day after Passover is done. Don't worry about getting your stuff now, we're gonna be late getting over to the station. I'll just drop you off at your apartment's lobby door, and then later I'll see ya inside the studio. I'll get all your stuff here cleaned up and pack a bag for myself. Then we'll stay at your place for the next few nights."

"Oh I forgot to tell you, I've got that meet and greet gig this evening, so you can just let yourself in. If you'll start on dinner, I'll be home around 9:30. Please keep it light, none of that heavy pasta of yours. By the way, let's eat out on the balcony."

As always with Lucy and Rico, any personal conversations came to an abrupt ending as they approached the studio's back door. However, some seventeen hours later, it continued without missing a beat.

"I'm telling you, your doorman knows what's going on with us."

"Are you kidding me? There are so many people cheating on each other in this building, why do you think they call it 'Peyton Place' towers?"

It was over dinner that the lighthearted banter continued.

"I take it no one living here cares if their cover is blown or if the spouse finds out."

"Well, I hope my cover's not blown. I don't want my boyfriend to find out, but I'm only fooling around with him for his money!"

"Well here's some news for you, you're barking up the wrong tree. It's not his it's his mothers. She's the one who has it all, the money that is."

"So, is your dad still around?"

"As beautiful as you are, he'd give you what ever you asked for, but then again, the money is still my moms."

"Wow, so your family sounds like mine; my mother ruled with an iron fist also."

Rico looked into Lucy's eyes and told her he would love to sit and hear all about her family. He would also enjoy hearing all about her years of growing up in Asia. He reminded her that other than hearing her talking briefly about a younger brother, he knew very little, if anything about her family.

"What's there to tell? My brother and I both came along very late in our parents' lives. They were 'older than dirt' when we showed up. Both of us were still very young when our parents passed away. The people of our village raised us; we were passed around from family to family."

"Lucy, when I lived in Korea, I saw things like that happen more than once. Sad how so many Americans think that life here is so bad."

"Everything's better here in the west. Why the hell do you think I fought tooth and nail to get myself over here?"

"Lucy, I'm glad we're starting to get closer to each other. Let me know when you want to start playing the fantasy games."

"How did you know I was into sadomasochism, or being a dominatrix?"

"That's sounds sexy, then I can dress up as a GI and you can dress up as my Geisha girl, how's that sound to you?"

"Let me make something clear to you! I don't know what went on twenty years ago with your girlfriends in South Korea, but you seem to be confused. Let me be very clear about something here. I am from Japan, not some other part of Asia! The Geisha and the kimono have nothing to do with sex! I personally have way too much respect for the art form to have it devalued. I would rather you think of me as just a common whore. Any virtue I may have once had was ripped away from me when I was still a child. There is a world of difference between a real Geisha and me. The one thing I learned before leaving Japan was that sex was a tool, nothing more than a way to obtain more power."

SEVEN

And when your children ask you, 'What does this ceremony mean?' you will tell them, 'It is the Passover sacrifice to the Lord, who passed over the houses of the Israelites in Egypt and spared our homes when He struck down the Egyptians.

Who would have guessed that Nic would grow up to be such a loving and helpful big brother? This would be proven numerous times over, as he, his baby sister Suzie, and their mother traveled back to Flatbush for the Passover. It truly was Delilah's hopes that Rico would have been able to join them, but after having to take time off last fall for his stay in the hospital, no one was expecting him to make this trip to New York. Delilah would never admit to it, but she was happy not to have to attend any of the holy days celebrations at her mother-in-law's apartment on the east side of Brooklyn. With regard to the hell and history within the Mancini family, Delilah thought it best to have a live-and-let-live attitude, and stay as far away as she could. She was so happy for Rico's dad, David, when he had Hannah served with divorce papers. Delilah believed in the saying 'what goes around, comes around.' Hannah got her just rewards, as she had been bitter toward David since 1944 when the family moved from Italian Harlem to what she thought of as the ghettos of Flatbush.

When Delilah told her family that Rico would not be in attendance this year, her mother was also somewhat grateful, yet being the wise woman she was, she expressed how sorry she would be at his absence.

This year's Passover would be no different than any other had been in the past. Flatbush's favorite Italian eatery closed its doors only 7 days per year. They were the first and last days of the high holy days, Fourth of July, Christmas Day and New Years Day.

They found it practical to close on Christmas Eve because everyone in the neighborhood thought a good Catholic family should close their restaurant early so they could attend midnight mass. As long as the Russo family had been on the corner of Erasmus Street and Bedford, little did anybody ever realize that although they were Italian, they were never going to be a good Catholic family!

Delilah always found it unique that while most people returned home for major family celebrations during November or December, her family gathered in the fall and spring each year. There may not have been any hot chocolate waiting for anyone as they entered the family's home and restaurant. However the reception was just as warm as if chestnuts had been roasting on an open fire.

As had been the case for as long as she could remember, Becca drove into the city the night before from Long Island, in order to help her mother with the preparations for the evening's feast.

She was looking forward to next year's Passover, not because she had grown accustomed over the years of doing a vast majority of the work, no it was because next year there would be no need for the drive at all.

Delilah's older sister, Rebekah Lynn and husband Matthew, were celebrating their first granddaughter who just arrived several months before Suzie was born. Rebekah Lynn and her sister Delilah were not the only two of the three Russo siblings to celebrate something special that year. Their brother Jacob, and his wife Ruth and children, were celebrating that their paperwork had just come back for Aliyah, their immigration to Israel. Jacob Russo, who was just a few weeks shy of his 37th birthday, had dreamed about someday moving to Israel. He also dreamed the day would come when the medical degree he spent so long working on obtaining would be put to use as he worked as a Doctor in Jerusalem.

The family, minus one older sister, Becca, was celebrating that he would now also be an official member of the 1972 Israeli Olympic Delegation. He would be working with the coaches as a medic and advisor. Becca, who had the ability to find a terrorist under every other rock, thought Israel shouldn't be participating in the Olympics in Germany.

She continued asking, "After only thirty years had they already forgotten the holocaust?" Jacob hadn't given it a second thought, and his wife and three kids would be staying in one of the hotels in Munich. He was ecstatic that he would be staying with the male members of the delegation in the Olympic village.

It's funny how men bond by insulting one another and, yet, they don't mean a word of it. Women, however, often compliment each other, and yet they too don't mean a word of it. Often times, when brothers have issues with one another, they give each other a black eye, and the next day they have grown closer. However, when it comes to sisters, it seems that one does everything and the other does nothing simply according to whom you might have asked. Delilah had not been home at the restaurant for a Passover in several years. So when she asked if she could help, she expected to hear Rebecca tell her 'no,' that she and mom had been doing it for so many years; it would be simpler for them to take care of it by themselves, and that she truly didn't need to bother! Oddly enough, that was not the case this year and because of this, Delilah felt all the more uneasy about the evening's festivities. Why she wasn't sure, but she just kept waiting for the 'other shoe' to drop.

Although Matthew wasn't a first-born he attended with his oldest son, Matt Jr. He told everyone just how odd it felt without Zaide.

"You know how crazy Pop's leadership in anything could be, much less the removal of the yeast from throughout the house."

He also said it was very solemn without Tony's wise cracks.

"I am so sorry Delilah; you must be going through hell, right about now, not knowing what happened. You know he came over every other week to sit and have lunch with mom. She is afraid to say anything to you. We all ache for you!"

"Becca, really it's okay, really it is. I mean, what's a wife and mother to do? My little Nicky walks around on eggshells; absolutely terrified he's about to say the wrong thing at the wrong time. Then there's his father, that bastard. That's it, when life get's tough, go and have yourself a stroke."

"Delilah, shut your mouth, are you crazy?"

"Becca, I just don't know anymore. What the hell is going on with my life? As for being crazy, I very well may be. Hell, a year ago I had both my parents. I was a happy middle-aged navy wife, with two kids, less than five years 'till I had an empty nest, and a husband who was thinking about retirement.

Now, I'm changing diapers for a ten-week-old infant, my twenty year old has just vanished into thin air, and my soon to be fifteen year old boy is the only thing close to normal in my life. Then there's that ass of a husband who thinks I'm too stupid to figure out he's hiding something from me. Sis, on second thought, damn it, yes, yes, yes, I am crazy! Crazy as a fruit cake."

"Speaking of crazy, it's a good crazy, do you want to know now, or wait and find out with everybody else at the dinner table tonight?"

"You're pregnant, and I'm not the only Russo girl that's insane."

"Bite your tongue, Delilah, shit, you are crazy!"

"So Becca, spill your guts about the big news."

"Let me go and get Mom, Jacob, and Matthew."

The Russo family gathered upstairs in the living room. Included were Mrs. Russo, the matriarch, along with her three children Jacob, Delilah, and Rebekah, Matthew Zuckermann Rebekah's husband, and the Russos' long time family attorney.

As Delilah's mom entered into the room, it hit her that the last time all five of these adults were in this room together, was when they all shared the responsibility of the Shomer, or the watchman over her father's body.

Jewish tradition says from death to burial the deceased should never be left alone. Before Mama Russo could be seated, Delilah's emotional state of being began to crumble, only to be followed by a hysterical fit of uncontrolled sobbing. This was the emotional breakdown that most of her family had long been waiting for her to have.

Matthew backed out of what had become the crying huddle, found his way down the stairs, and started looking for Jacob's wife Ruthie, who passed little Suzie off to Becca's oldest daughter. Matthew then found Nic, and asked them both to come upstairs. It didn't take Nic long to realize what was going on, and was mindful not to say anything about Tony. He and the rest of the family reassured his mother that someday all would be okay! As King David wrote, "Weeping may stay for the night, but rejoicing comes in the morning." There must have been some truth to it, because shortly after the crying finally subsided, laughter erupted.

In hopes of using the laughter as a means by which to continue, Matthew looked at Mama Russo and asked if the defense could approach the bench for a sidebar. He turned to Delilah and told her that a family forum had been reached and the consensus was to be announced at dinner. No one wanted Delilah to feel as though she had been blindsided.

Mathew told her, "With Papa's passing shortly after last year's Passover, I was gonna host the Seder this year. However, when we all realized that Jacob, Ruthie, and the boys may not be stateside for a while, we decided to pass it over to him."

"That's fine by me. I think Papa would have liked that. So what's the big deal?"

Mama cleared her throat, and waved her arms about as if she were Moshe or Moses himself. She managed to part the family members in such a way that she was able to look Delilah in the face only to tell her, "The times, they are a changing. Let me tell you the news myself, then we are all going to find some place to take a nice little nap before all the guests start to show up."

Delilah asked, "All the guests, what guests?"

Rebekah answered, "Delilah, your nephews and nieces have spent this afternoon transforming the restaurant's dining room into a banquet hall. Ma, you wanna tell her?"

"The truth is, baby girl, the restaurant was your Pop's. It was his life. I only supported him in it. You and yours are trying to make lives for yourselves down in Virginia, and that is a good thing. Your brother and his bride are going home to Israel, and I love them for it. So, if your sister and her husband are gonna get stuck with the old lady, why not move me out to the country?

Matthew's law firm is rolling in the dough, and he has already had an addition built onto their house. This year will be our last Passover here in the city, and we are going out with a bang!"

"Rebekah, thank you for taking such good care of Mom, but then you always have, and done a damn good job. My only question is, will the Mancini family be invited to the island for Passover next year?"

"I'll think about it. I'm only joking; your family is always welcome in my home!"

Ask anyone living in a kosher home what is the first thing you did after the sun set on a Saturday evening, and they would tell you it was to turn on the television. While both her mother and son argued as to whether it was to be 'The Mary Tyler Moore Show' or 'The Streets of San Francisco' that night, Delilah had something more important on her mind. With Becca and her branch of the family tree back on Long Island, Delilah found herself locked away in what was once her papa's office. She called her sister, and hoped she might have the time for a nice long heart-to-heart. Although the term epiphany is so often associated with Catholicism, Delilah had what she could only describe as being the truest epiphany ever.

"I don't know Delilah, are you sure you're not just grasping at straws or something?"

"I don't know, but I did some digging, and his medical records showed that he was prescribed a hell of a lot of penicillin while he was in Korea. Much more than most others might have been."

"Delilah, he was also in a war zone for God's sake!"

"Okay, you wanna tell me how it takes two hours to get from the base to navy housing when we were at Pearl Harbor? Hell, we weren't even on the big island!"

"Well, okay, what else do you have?"

"Hell, if I had any tangible evidence to prove what I feel in my heart, your husband and I would have already started working on alimony and child support payments! Hold on, Nicky is at the door. Listen, mom has fallen asleep, and Nic can't get Suzie to settle down. You gonna be up for a while? Good, I'll call ya back in a bit. Love ya!"

It was the next morning when Nic realized something was out of order. His grandmother served his favorite breakfast, cheese blintzes. The strange thing was that she had always saved them for the last day of Passover, and yet there were still three more days to go. After he had finished his meal, his mother encouraged him to give Mama Russo all the loving he could. Delilah then told Nic they were going to be departing several days earlier than expected.

"Nicky, I'm going to have to tell a major lie to get us back on that plane three days early. I want you to wear your 'tallit katan and make sure all four of the tassels show, and wear your blue and white yarmulke. I need you to look like you just walked out of a Synagogue when we get on that airplane."

As Nic and his mother got out of the taxicab, he watched as she did something he'd never seen her do before. She pulled a long piece of silk from her pocket, tied her hair up with it, but also wrapped it around part of her face and neck.

As they walked into the airport she leaned over to him and told him from now on out it's Hebrew or nothing, no Italian, and definitely no English. She looked him in the eye and reminded him of all the things their people had been through over the years. She told him again, as if he didn't already know it, but most of the craziness took place during the Holy days, and if not in Israel, it would happen in New York City.

It was after she finished begging the ticket agent in a broken English, Yiddish and Hebrew mix, that she was then given two new tickets to return to Norfolk, without a costly penalty. It was also at that moment Nic realized as he watched Delilah, just where his brother's talents for acting really came from. He walked away from the ticket counter with only one thought. Why?

EIGHT

After walking through the house, Delilah found a soft plum lip stain on a wine glass sitting on the nightstand, next to what was once their marriage bed. Along with the two glasses of unfinished wine, she found a bathrobe several sizes too small to have been hers. She was now, more than ever before, ready to call her brother-in-law; ready to start some kind of proceedings! Her emotions ran the gamut. Would she ignore him, or should she destroy him? Was it to be revenge, or would she simply walk away? All she knew was he had left behind enough evidence for her to see him in a whole new light. If it was a goy he wanted, let him have her. Maybe it was time for Delilah to do the same thing. Had Delilah gotten to that point where she was ready to go out and find a young man with a big ole schmuck? That really wasn't her style, at least not yet. After jokingly thinking about her 'would be' gigolo, she found herself asking several very serious questions. What was a mother of two, to do? Stay in it for the sake of the kids? Her next thought was to return to the safety and comfort of her childhood home. Suddenly she remembered that was soon to be nothing more than a memory.

When it came down to personal heroes, Delilah had her three ladies that she could very easily place upon the proverbial pedestal. Eva Peron, Lady Godiva, and last but certainly not lest, Golda Meir, the Iron Lady of Israel, and current Prime Minister. As much as these women put their people ahead of themselves,

Delilah liked them because they never let the lack of money keep them down. They made their way into the history books, not because of their husbands, but in spite of them.

One of them had to change her name, another had to change her tactics and the third simply changed her clothes. Now that Delilah knew in her heart what the truth was, she wondered what she would have to change in order for her to go forward?

It was with the insertion of a key into the dead bolt along with it's turning that she realized the spring afternoon had become evening. She only had a moment to decide what to do. With Nicky growing up so quickly, she couldn't tell them apart through the opaque door. Was it Rico, or Nicky? Should she hide everything from his young eyes, protect him, or tell him what she could no longer deny? The question was whether it was time for him to learn the truth about his family, or just his father.

"Mom, where have you been? I've been calling you forever; didn't you hear the telephone ringing? What's wrong, you look like you've seen a ghost; is something wrong?"

"What makes you think there's anything wrong?"

"Come on, Mom, let's get real, nothing has been right in a long, long time. I know this has been a hard year on everybody with Zaide and Tony being gone, but you have never left a Passover early, never! And when did you start letting the phone ring off the hook? Ma, with all those temple ladies you may be one of the best storytellers of all times, but give me a break. I know you're not telling me the truth, not this time."

"Okay kid, you've got me dead to rights. Truth be told, I was questioning if I should just break down and tell you everything, or try and rise above it all, and keep it to myself. Nicky, I think it's time to let you know what's been going on with your mom and dad. Are you hungry, hell, you're always hungry! Let me go upstairs and check Suzie's diaper. When I get back down, we can get some hummus and matzos, then sit and have a nice long talk! Did I really just say that? I swear I'm getting old. I'm turning into your grandma."

"Mom, forgive me, but are you, you know, um, drunk?"

"I don't know if I would say drunk. I'm okay to change a diaper, but I'm not about to drive a car, that's for sure!"

"Mom, please tell me what's wrong?"

"All in good time, my son." With Delilah going up the stairs, Nic thought about what the hell he was about to find himself in the midst of.

"Well now, that didn't take long at all. She's still dry, so let's get this party going, shall we."

"Mom, are you sure you wanna open this can of worms in front of me?"

"The parent in me wants to say that everything is just fine, practically perfect in every way! It's the little girl in me who wants to tell you, your Abba, yes, your father; he is nothing more than a meshugener. Maybe this is not such a good idea after all! Do you want to know what the truth of the matter is? Hell boy, I think I'm just about tipsy enough to talk to you just the way I would your brother. But do you want to hear any of this crap?"

"Well, I'm not really sure what to say to that one. Should I be honored you're tipsy enough to let down your guard? Do I finally get the truth, or is it that you're desperate enough to start using me as your sounding board like you did with Tony?"

"Tony, that is rude, and uncalled for."

"Tony, Tony, well the cat's out of the bag now, isn't it? Just in case you forgot, my name is Nic, not Nicky, it's just Nic. Also can you please tell me why it's always been about you and Tony? Why am I always put on the back burner? Am I too intelligent, too stoic, what? Have you ever thought I might miss my fratello also?"

"Nicky, Nic, you're right, I've been too short-sighted. Calm down young man, get a hold of yourself!"

"Mom, I miss him too! Don't you understand? I've always loved him. I always loved it that he never treated me special. When we did speak on the phone he acted like I was as dumb as the rest of his friends. And Ma, I love ya, but for once can we forego all the niceties? Please just call it what it is. Mishegas, what calling something by its Yiddish name is going to make it any better? Dad has never held back, why should you? Okay let's see, according to my parents, my mom is a bitch, and my dad is an ass! Finally, I'm a normal American teenager!"

"So, I'm a bitch, am I?"

"Mom, you're missing the point. He said you were often on the 'bitchy' side, and you called him 'stupid and crazy.' I just helped you say what you were thinking, that's all."

"No, here's the point. You, my son, are too sober for us to have any conversation, and I'm too drunk to keep from telling you the truth."

"Mom, that's the whole point of alcohol, to allow you the freedom to say what needs to be said. Not that I know personally, but I have heard it said that 'drunken minds speak sobering thoughts.'"

It was over the next several hours that the two of them spoke with one another, as they had never spoken before. Nic, growing up in an Italian household had never been denied a glass of wine, if he had ever wanted it. However, he knew better. It was his father's voice he heard in the back of his head, telling him that it was 'loose lips that sank ships.' He always added to that he shouldn't go around telling everyone everything he knew. Even though he was speaking with his mother, his plan was not to let all of Tony's secrets out of the bag. In what seemed to be no more than an hour, the conversation came to a close. As a result of that late night talk, Delilah and Nic's relationship changed forever. Going forward, the dynamics of the Mancini family also changed that night. In their hearts and minds, they went from being a family of five, to a family of three.

# # #

As much as some may have called him a dog, Rico tucked his tail between his legs and found his way across the street to lick his wounds at the 'Recovery Room', the bar across from both her apartment and the radio station. At 2 a.m., Rico found himself closing the bar then with nowhere else to go he called a cab. Rico not being the most patience of people, gave his opinion on just how slow the cabbies where in this town, and then yelled his address at him. "746 Graydon Avenue please." He returned home to find quite a surprise awaiting him. Rico almost tripped on it as he entered the front door. It was a small box containing a kimono styled bathrobe, a set of wine glasses, and a note.

Dearest Rico,

You may think of me as still being that nice little Jewish girl. Or maybe you see me as just an Old Italian woman. I am, both of those things; however, I am so much more than that.

I have brought three children into this world. I've got no problem taking one foolish old man out of it! You kapish?

Delilah

It was Rico's dad, David Mancini, who taught him that when the little lady finds out you have screwed up. You take your tongue-lashing, on the chin. Then you take her to the best high end place you can find. She may deserve to make a fool out of you and herself. After all you did, or she wouldn't be so pissed at you. Take your medicine like a man, and if you're lucky she might let you off with only a warning.

"I was wrong, DeeDee, and I know it. Please let me take you to dinner and we can talk about it."

"Why on God's green earth would I want to go with you and talk about anything?"

"DeeDee, I said I was wrong. Have you never made a mistake, got caught up in the moment?"

"Okay, I've made a mistake or two, one may have been marrying you. But if you think you can take me to one of the places where you took her, forget it, I'll know."

Delilah quickly called Annie and Betty to ask if either one would stay with Suzie while she prepared herself for an evening of Rico eating crow and her serving him a very large slice of humble pie.

As the evening progressed, the Mancinis reset the ground rules for the remainder of their marriage. Delilah spoke volumes to Rico with her monotone voice, and coldness in her eyes. The message Rico received was simple enough; I will love you 'till the day I die. However he knew one more indiscretion it would be over! She went so far as to add that she would release the wrath of Hell itself on him, and only the creator of Heaven and Earth could see him through it.

Over the course of the next several months nothing much changed, except the hours of the day, and the days of the week. Passover gave way to Mother's Day, followed by Nic's fifteenth birthday, and eventually Father's Day. Five weeks later came the date the family had been dreading as though it were the plague itself. July 30, 1972 should have been a happy occasion, the one year anniversary of living in southeastern Virginia, sadly it was anything but. It had been a year unlike any other, and with all she had been through, Delilah would never blame moving to the quaint little seaside city of Norfolk for what had come to her family.

Several weeks later, while attending the WJDC Labor Day picnic on Stockley Gardens, the inquisition began to unfold. When Elizabeth got her hands on little Suzie, a fun-filled day in the park turned into a nightmare.

Delilah had noticed, over the last several weeks, that Suzie seemed to be off her game just a wee bit.

"Delilah, I'm sure it's nothing, but has Suzie been sick or had a cold lately?"

"Well no, she hasn't, why do you ask?"

"Were your boys a little slow when it came to putting on weight their first year? I know we girls tend to be a little more delicate, but at eight months..."

"Liz, get to the point, you're starting to frighten me."

"It's just that she seems so petite and lethargic for a baby her age!"

The next day Delilah took Suzie to Portsmouth Naval Hospital. During the battery of tests, Delilah saw everything in a whole new light. Never once did Suzie jump, cry, try to pull away...nothing. She just lay there as the nurses drew her blood and as the doctor checked her ears, eyes and then checked her throat. That afternoon the hospital called and set a follow up appointment for the following morning.

"Tell me, Mr. and Mrs. Mancini, with a name like Mancini, are both of you Italian? It must confuse some people as to your family's heritage."

Rico asked, "What do you mean?"

"I don't want to stereotype, but I happened to see in your family records you are Jewish, correct?"

"Again, Doc, where are you going with this?"

"Are you sure you are both Italian, and not maybe Russian, or Eastern European? It wouldn't matter; it's a moot point. The results have come in and well, I'm so sorry but your daughter has 'The Jewish Fur Trader Hypothesis'."

Delilah let out a blood-curdling scream.

"No! Don't you dare, don't you say it!"

Rico looked at both DeeDee then at the doctor, with a facial expression that said it all.

"Forgive me, Doc, but I don't understand! What are you saying to us?"

Mr. Mancini I am so sorry, but your little girl has Tay-Sachs."

As the doctor started to explain, to Rico, Delilah cried out in Hebrew then from nowhere she reached up just above her heart and ripped her favorite lightweight sweater. Without another word, Rico knew deep in his heart what just happened.

The doctor had just pronounced a death sentence over his little baby girl. He then dropped to his knees and cried.

"There is no refuge from memory and remorse in this world. The spirits of our foolish deeds haunt us, with or without repentance."

NINE

Tony truly knew in his head that the new city he was to call home was beautiful, with the palm trees, and the warm breezes. He also knew he was lucky to have a new job where he got paid to sing all day. However in his heart, he had resigned himself to believed he would never love again, or at least find himself in a relationship with another man.

"7 2 Q Y V this is Daniel Miller, 7 2 Q Y V Daniel Miller here, good morning, come back."

"Danny, why on earth are you up at this ungodly hour? You must be crazy; we could have slept in for several more hours. But where do I find you? Out here playing on that silly radio of yours."

"Well good morning sunshine, Reuben, nobody told you to get out of bed. Don't tell me you missed me, Mr. Esposito, I don't think it's sleeping you wanted more of, something tells that you just want to have your way with my body?"

"Yeah, right old man."

"Ouch Reuben, that hurt, and who are you calling old? I'm only 29."

"Twenty-nine, my ass, Danny; come back to bed."

"What was that, you said Cocoa Beach is just waiting for us, and it's less than an hour's drive away. It's the first Wednesday after Labor Day. It might be locals only this morning."

"Danny, if you want to keep this young man happy, you'll get back in bed with me."

"I'm on my way to the head, let me hit the shower and I'll see you in two minutes."

"Thank goodness, some men do listen when they're told what to do! We have ourselves a genius," Reuben said. "Danny, no wonder they hired you to work as one of the tunnel rats. You truly are a genius."

Yelling from the bedroom as he packed a bag for both Reuben and himself, Danny asked if he had a choice.

"You can invite me into the shower with you, and kill two birds with one stone. Then we can drive over to the beach. Danny, I understand why you live for getting out into the sunshine. It would drive me crazy being one of you tunnel rats! Working down there all day with all those computers and animatronics and sound sensors, and never seeing the light of day? I really love what I do, but think I'm ready for a bit of a getaway!"

Danny brought out the bag he had packed before getting into the shower. All the while the conversation continued.

"Well, let's get away for a few days. We both have the time. Where do you want to go? The Castro in San Francisco, DuPont Circle in D.C., or how about Greenwich Village in New York?" asked Danny.

"Danny, I want to go to San Francisco, my love, let's go west ..." Danny, who had long ago perfected the 'Navy shower', was in and out in a matter of a minute or two. However, when he exited the bathroom he expected to find Ruben on the bed, and to continue the conversation about traveling west.

As he walked down the hall, heading towards the living room, he heard what sounded like a very static filled commercial radio broadcast. Danny saw Reuben sitting, totally engaged, as if the voice on the short wave radio, was talking to Ruben only.

"So Reuben, is he giving away the secrets to life? What's he saying that's got you so engrossed? What was that, he said the fountain of youth was where? What's up babe?"

"Shut up! Oh my Lord, turn on the television, now! Damn it, they've done it to us again! There's been a massacre in Munich, Germany! Eleven members of the Israeli team have been shot. Why, why Yahweh? Why do they always want to kill us?"

As the gray, grainy television picture slowly grew brighter and clearer, a black and white image of a popular sports reporter spoke in a very emotional voice, informing his viewing audience of the following information.

"Ladies and gentlemen, this is Tim McCray reporting. As of 3:24 a.m., Munich time, we received confirmation and our worst fears have been realized tonight. There were eleven hostages; two were killed in their rooms yesterday morning and the remaining nine were killed tonight at the airport. Yes, they're all gone."

As Mr. McCray finished his report, the names of all eleven scrolled down, as the seventh name appeared on the screen, Reuben let out a cry of pure anguish. He found himself clinging to Danny, and sobbing uncontrollably over the loss of his one and only uncle, Jacob Russo.

As much as Daniel Miller felt he knew by his third date that the man who called himself Reuben truly could be trusted, he also knew that for whatever the reason, a wall of privacy had been built up. He also knew it was never going to be lowered, never! It was with his propensity to over-analyze anything and everything Danny finally got it right. He knew enough to simply stand there and offer his support; support that was needed by one he loved.

#

Delilah answered the phone having no knowledge of the tragedies going on outside her small little hamlet. That is why she was so startled to hear her sister's voice speaking the Kaddish because she had not yet told anyone about little Suzie's diagnosis.

"Kaddish, may His great name be blessed forever, and to all eternity."

"Becca, is that you? How did you know already? We haven't told anyone yet."

"Told anyone? The whole world knows, Delilah. It's the only thing on the news
since last night."

"What are you talking about?"

"Haven't you heard the news? Sit down. I have some tragic news to tell you. Are
you sitting yet?"

"Yes, but what's going on?"

"Well, there's no easy way to tell you this, but Jacob's gone. I am sorry to be the one to tell you, but our fratello, along with ten others, were killed yesterday."

"What the hell are you saying? I just can't take this right now. I will not hear this, no, not today! Sis, I just can't handle all this, not today, oh God help me!"

"What the hell is going on with you? I hear it in your voice, something is terribly wrong with you."

"Oh my, yeah it is, but Jacob, how the hell, dead are you sure, how's Mom? Are you sure?"

"Yeah honey, I'm sorry, it's Jacob; he's dead. What's going on with you?"

"My Lord how's Mom? Can Mom hear you talking with me? Becca, how did this happen? I just knew you or I would go first!"

"Mom is lying down. She is trying to grasp what happened. You need to turn on the TV to catch up with the rest of us. I just called to find out if you and the kids would be going? If we're gonna make it, we need to fly out as soon as we can."

"Flying? Where? What are you talking about?"

"You need to get up here, then we'll probably fly to Paris, and then straight to Tel Aviv. Delilah, I can give you just a few more minutes to think about it. Matt is ready to call and book our flight. But, I ask you again, what is going on with you? What caused your hesitation? What made Jacob's death pale in comparison? Delilah, are you still there?"

Picking up the kitchen telephone, and not hearing a dial tone, Nic asked if anyone was on the phone.

"Nicky, it's your Aunt Becca. Find your mom and tell her I need to speak with her! Time is of the essence."

"Mom, Aunt Becca is on the phone for you. Mom, pick up the phone!"

As quick as he could, Nic ran up the stairs to find his mother sitting in the floor with tears running down her checks. He pulled the receiver out of her hand, and then shook her shoulder.

"Ma, hey, Ma, Aunt Becca needs to talk with you!"

"Oh Becca, I am at such a loss as to what to do."

"Delilah, I need to know, and don't let the lack of money make the decision for you. Sis, it's okay, Matthew and I have the airfare. Are you ready to travel? Is everyone's passport in order?"

"Passports? Slow down, let me get downstairs and turn on the TV. I can't leave Suzie, not now."

"Are your passports still valid? No one is asking you to leave Suzie, she is still young enough to fly without papers."

"I don't think I could make it to the end of the block today, much less the other side of the world."

"What on earth has happened? I just spoke with Nicky, so it must be Rico or Suzie."

"We weren't gonna tell anyone 'till we spoke to another pediatrician, a civilian doctor at the hospital just up the street."

"Oh dear Lord, what's wrong with Suzie?"

"It's baby Adam all over again!"

"Oh, sweet Lord, why?"

"Becca, you're the first one I have told. Again, how's Mom doing?"

"Mom's lying down; she's putting on a brave face, but I can see it in her eyes, she's numb."

"My goodness, has anyone spoken to Ruthie? What about the boys?"

"Where is the memorial taking place?"

"Tel Aviv."

"Are you crazy, going there just days before the start of Rosh Hashanah?"

"It's not like I picked out the day I thought my brother should be shot and killed!"

"That place will be like a powder keg. Oh my goodness, I don't think I can do it right now."

"I'm not strong enough for Mom. I'll be a burden to all of you right now. Give my love to Mama for me. You and Matt be strong for both her and Ruth, and tell the kids I love them. Shalom."

Standing behind his mother Nic tapped her on the shoulder and asked, "Mom, who is baby Adam?"

"Oh Lord God, not this morning, Nic, not today, please not today."

"Mom, didn't we sit at the dining room table not too long ago, and swear to tell the truth, no matter how hard it was?"

"I can't think of a better way to spend the Thursday morning before Rosh Hashanah, than telling my son the facts of life."

"Mom, I already know about the birds and the bees. Dad told me, well tried to tell me all about it."

"No, my boy, the facts are simple; there are hateful people on this planet, death is a part of life, and there will always be deep family secrets."

"Mom, I don't get it."

"Okay, you want the truth? Let me make it easy for you. Don't tell the goyim, but there's no Great Pumpkin, there's no Easter Bunny, and no Santa Claus. You wanna know what else? The topper is that only the good die young. My baby brother, Adam, was taken at the age of only three and a half!"

"Mom, you don't have a brother named Adam!"

"I guess now is as good time as any, Nicky, it's called a family secret for a reason. I love you, but you don't know it all. I do have a second brother, He would be, oh my, about six years older than Tony, had he lived."

"Why didn't you tell me?"

"Listen young man! Do you think I go around telling everybody I meet every little thing I know? What, should I stop people on the street? Did you know that my oldest boy is as queer as a three dollar bill, or that the family genius is also Dr. Jekyll and sometimes he's Mr. Hyde?

Or that my husband is still out there fucking around on me! Oh, here's one more for good measure, my one and only daughter is going to die in less than three years? No, sometimes Nic, you just take these things with you to the grave."

TEN

Nic's first year in public high school was just as boring as any he had attended in San Diego. According to him, the only interesting part about the school was the person that the school was named after, Commodore Matthew Fontaine Maury, a naval officer. Then again, that seemed to be the way in both San Diego and Norfolk; everything was named after something related to the navy.

Yoshi Suzuki and Nic Mancini became newfound friends. It was odd the way they met, not in algebra or chemistry class, but in an art appreciation class. It turned out that they both liked the works of Spanish surrealist Salvador Dali. In little more than a week, the two had become fast friends. According to Mei, Yoshi's sister, the two were the geekiest guys in school.

After Delilah met Yori and Hachi, Yoshi's parents, and their older boy Taro, she saw a similarity between herself and Mei. Different birth order, yet it was three siblings growing up in an apartment above the family restaurant. And if that wasn't enough, the restaurant was located across the street from the neighborhood high school.

Delilah found it strange, yet ever so funny that she'd never been drawn to any of the ladies at the Temple. Yet, within two weeks of meeting Hachi, she knew she had found a kindred spirit in her.

She knew Annie, being several years her junior, would always be a surrogate big sister. Hachi was more like one of the little girls back in the old country, which her mother would have Becca and Delilah pray for.

This thought was confirmed one morning when Hachi, along with several other ladies, explained about their families being held in the American Japanese Internment Camps when they were children. Delilah was shocked, having never been taught about any other cultures other than her own. To hear just how long and hard these ladies road was during the war. As much as Delilah's distant family knew all too well about the ghettos and death camps. She, like so many other Americans, knew nothing about what happened in the western states during the dark days of World War II.

As the tea party started to unfold in front of Delilah, Hachi stepped in to teach her what to do, and when it was done, as the other ladies would not leave Delilah out. That morning she was reminded, regardless of race, creed, or color, women the world over have been helping one another through the ages of time with a shoulder to cry on, or as this morning, a friend to laugh with.

"So, how long have you all known one another?" asked Delilah of the ladies sitting at the table.

"Since the beginning of time, give or take a few decades."

"Delilah," Hachi asked, "See those two really old fat women? That would be my mother- n-law on the left, and her much, much younger, skinnier sister."

Seconds later, the skinnier woman responded to her sister, "Old woman, be quiet will you please, you know she's right. There's dirt that's younger than you are."

Hachi continued, "Then there are these three lovely young ladies who have worked the lunch rush forever."

"Hachi, did they all grow up in the internment camps together with you?"

"Delilah, forgive my laughter. I forget most people think we all look the same, Asian people, that is. The entire Suzuki family is from southern Japan, however, Zhaoyang and her sisters are from a province in northern China. We laugh at the fact that a Japanese family runs a Chinese restaurant. Maybe one day the Japanese style of cooking will be more widely accepted."

As had become the weekly tradition, Yori stepped out of the kitchen long enough to let all the ladies know it was time to close down the tea party, and start the work week.

Yori made it his newest tradition to find out how things were going for his son's best friend, along with his wife's newest girlfriend. Nic Mancini, Yori's new foster son, never meaning to, brought it to his attention that things back home at the Mancini household were not at all happy go lucky, as they once were.

Never wanting to make Delilah lose face, the Suzuki's would have never repeated any of what they had overheard from Nic about his home life. Yori, whose name simply meant 'Trust,' knew a thing or two about building the bonds of trust.

One Sunday morning in early October, he gathered up his family into the station wagon and drove over to the Mancini house. After begging Delilah, she and her two young ones joined them, they all enjoyed breakfast at The Donut House. Since none of the seven guests of The Donut House were true southerners, they talked each other into trying what some say is the best thing about breakfast down South, grits. Delilah actually ate a second helping, along with some bacon; so did several other members of the breakfast party.

As early October turned into mid-December, the four local members of the Suzuki family, and the three sociable Mancini members, became best friends. Delilah had once like so many other Jewish mothers, hoped to one-day find that perfect, little Jewish girl for her son Nicky. From where she sat now, she realized that love was so much more important than any cultural custom could ever be! Her hopes changed that someday he would simply meet the right girl. Who knew? Maybe one day, she might live to see the Suzuki and Mancini families joined together by marriage.

Outside of wartime, this was going to be the first year; the Mancini family would not be together for New Year's Eve. The Suzukis never had the chance to befriend Rico, and were already building bonds with Delilah. As a result they invited Delilah and the kids to their home.

Maybe it was time for Delilah to say goodbye to some old traditions. Those traditions dictated that you had to be at your husband's side to celebrate the Gentile's New Year. Last year's Rosh Hashanah was bad enough as it issued in Rico's stroke, and this year was far worse, with the news of her baby girl Suzie's terminal illness. Maybe some how, some way, standing on the sidelines watching the Suzuki family bring in the New Year with all the old Japanese ways, might turn out to be best.

#

Delilah dragged herself out of her bed early on Sunday yelling, "Who on God's green earth is making all that noise this early in the morning? I thought the Suzukis weren't coming over till sometime after church."

"Mom, come on downstairs."

"I know there is no way Annie would come over before church was over either. Whoever it is, I'm gonna kill them for waking me up!"

All the while Nic continued yelling for his mother's attention.

"Mother! Get down here now and say good morning to..."

"Would you hold your horses for just a moment."

As she descended the stairs, she rubbed her eyes in disbelief.

"Becca, Mother, what on earth are you two doing down here? Why didn't you let me know you were coming? Why are you here? What's going on? Are Matthew and the kids okay?"

"Delilah Russo Mancini, are you truly that forgetful? If you would stop running your mouth and take a breath, I will remind you of a few things. What is happening in just two days? You are going to stick to traditions, aren't you? You know the party is always on the Sunday nearest their special day. Also, how often does a girl turn one?"

"Mom, it wasn't really necessary for you two to come all the way down here for that. When did your flight arrive?"

"Oh, we got in last night and just stayed at some motel down the street from the airport. Where is that little granddaughter of mine?"

"Oh, Mom, she's still in bed, and needs to be changed."

"She's not the first grandchild I have changed, and won't be my last, right Nicky?"

Nic reminded his grandmother that if she were making a reference to his someday having a child, it would be a great grandchild and wouldn't happen for a while.

"Nic, take your grandmother up and show her where everything is kept."

As soon as Mamma Russo had gotten half way up the stairs, Delilah grabbed her sister's arm and pulled her into the kitchen.

"What the hell is going on? How much did you tell her?"

She hadn't told their mother anything about what was going on in Delilah's world. She then reminded her that their mother, tended to know things before they happened.

"Delilah Marie Russo, what the hell is going on up here? What's wrong with my grandchild?"

"Mom, I've asked that very same question for almost sixteen years now."

"Cut the crap, do you hear me? Young lady, I have seen that look before! Jacob isn't the only child I have lost. She has it, doesn't she, well doesn't she?"

"Mom, oh God Mom, yes she has it. I wish I could say no, but that would just be a lie. I keep hoping, but we know the truth, there is no hope for her."

"Hell, I thought I taught you two girls, with our blood, you could never fool around with an eastern European."

"Mom, Rico's a southern..."

"Girl, Rico is an ass if ever there was one! This child's father was from Eastern Europe. Don't try and lie to me! I've lost two of my boys, a grandson, and now I'm going to lose my youngest granddaughter. Rebekah Lynn, how long have you known about this?"

"Honestly, Mom, I don't know."

"Honestly, honestly, I am not that naive! Becca you wouldn't know honest if it slapped you on the back of the head! You wanna try again?"

"Mom, please, it's all my fault, not Becca's. I should have told you, it's just that, well, you had just lost Jacob. Mom, I didn't think you could take it, I'm sorry."

"No, baby, I'm sorry for you. Welcome to the very depths of hell itself. There is nothing like putting your babies in the ground. At least I know where mine have been laid to rest.

You still don't know anything about your baby Tony, do you? Come here, baby, let it out, you know I'm still your momma."

# # #

As had become the custom, Delilah sat there and ate a large bowl of sticky rice stolen from the Sushi chef. She also asked the same rhetorical question repeatedly of Hachi.

Then out of the blue one day she received an answer. One she had never expected, never in a million years.

"Oh Hachi, what the hell am I gonna do? I told him I would leave him if I ever caught him fooling around on me. He swore to me he would never cheat again. What's worse, I truly believed him. How stupid can a person be?"

"Did you mean it?" asked Hachi.

"What do you mean?"

"Delilah, it's a simple question, did you mean it? You know, did you really mean you would leave him, or was it just talk?"

"I don't know what I meant."

"And he knows it! Maybe it is time to leave him."

"Are you crazy? That's easy for you to say, you have the perfect life. How long have you and Yori been together? Come on, you two are the perfect Christian family, with your three perfect children."

"Delilah, I have never said I was perfect, nor have I lived the perfect life. Can I let you in on a little secret?"

"Yeah? What?"

"Well, my first husband fooled around with a married woman for three years before I learned about it. I didn't find out until I overheard two so-called friends talking about it in the restroom at church one Sunday morning. I thought I was going to vomit right then and there."

"Oh my goodness, you've got to be kidding me."

"No, I wish I could say it was all a joke, but what I thought was going to send me over the edge, was when I found out who she was. It was my best girlfriend. We grew up together. What's even worse, and I am only telling you this because I really believe you need to hear it, not only was she my best girlfriend, but also Yori's first wife, and Taro's birth mother."

"What on earth did you all do?"

"I won't even say her name anymore, but she gave up custody of Taro so she could run around with her new boyfriend, my ex, but you know what, karma's a bitch. No really, what you sow, you shall reap!

She left him behind, got involved with drugs, and I understood she bottomed out and turned to prostitution. He turned his life around and returned to the church, but Yori and I, as odd as it may sound, found our way out here with his family, and it's been wonderful."

"Delilah, how do you know he's fooling around on you again?"

"I know him well enough, and he can't keep it to himself. If he's not giving it to me, he's giving it to someone somewhere; that much I know to be true. Aside from that, I smelled her perfume on him the other day. I first got a whiff of it on her the night of the New Year's Eve party. It's a rather common fragrance back in Hawaii and California. She's the only person I've met since we returned to the east coast who wears Patchouli."

ELEVEN

"Miss Chue, I am so glad you had the wisdom to meet with me, as opposed to my having to chase you down and show up at your and my husband's workplace! I say my husband because that is still what he is, at least for the moment. I feel it's only fair to explain myself to you. Sometimes I come across as the tall, skinny, unsophisticated, big mouthed, stupid Italian."

"Miss Chue, let me say this, although I'm sure you already know this. Most men are stupid, mine included. They let the little head make all the big decisions. I think I have figured you out. Unlike most Asian women, you have no honor! You are a cold-hearted snake in the grass. I am just the one to cut you down!"

"Mrs. Mancini, I don't know where this..."

"Don't interrupt me. I want you to look back and know that you were warned. Yeah, he still has some steam in his locomotive, but you could do so much better for yourself. The money you thought he had all belongs to my 16-year-old son and nobody can touch it. As for Rico's retirement, you do know he was enlisted, and not an officer."

"Mrs. Mancini, I don't want to take your husband...!"

"Shut up! I don't want him back. I will not fight you for him. Understand this, I have lost two children, a brother, and now a husband. I don't have much fight left in me. Here's something Rico may have forgotten to tell you, my side of the family is like a dog with a bone, and they never give up.

With the recent loss of our brother, we, my sister, brother-in-law, and I, have yet to find a place to put our anger. We are the worst of the worst, we're New York City Jews.

As the kids say nowadays, your ass is grass, and my family, hell we are the lawnmowers, if you will! I will take the greatest pleasure in cutting you down! Or at least watching my lawyers do so."

It wasn't 48 hours later that Delilah's brother-in-law was introducing her to his college roommate. When she spoke to Matthew and told him just how crazy her world had become over the last year, he promised to send her the very best of the best, and that is just what he did. The afternoon Mr. Johnny Westbrook knocked on Delilah's door was like none other. She had found her knight in shining armor.

Although she had never heard the term before, it sounded perfect when Mr. Westbrook told her what he planed to sue for. Alienation of affection was the charge, he told Delilah he had no reason to believe it would not stand in a court of law.

"Mrs. Mancini, your brother-in-law Matthew gave me some basic information, but I have to ask a lot more personal questions. Before going before the judge tomorrow, I want to make sure I've got all of this straight."

It didn't take Mr. Westbrook and Delilah much more than an hour to go through all the information he would need to hang Miss Chue out to dry.

# # #

Over time, Reuben and Danny's relationship had grown rockier than the shores at Big Sue.

"I'm sorry Danny, but maybe it's time to trade me in for a more subservient model."

"Subservient?"

"I know it's a big word for someone as simple as me. I know my only skill is singing and dancing. And for the life of me I can't figure out why our employer has hired so many of us entertainers. All they really need are you computer gurus, right?"

"Where is all this coming from?"

"I love ya, but what the hell do you expect? Come on Danny, you are one of the smartest geeks in all America, and I'm just a pretty face and a good lay. A nice piece of ass!"

"Reuben, who the hell pissed in your corn flakes this morning?"

As the last word cane out of Danny's mouth, he felt the full wrath of Reuben. He went on to let Danny know that inside the work camp he very well may be a member of the Nazis party, and Reuben was just one of it's many prisoner. He went on to list the difference between their working conditions. He reminded Danny of his 9 to 5 Monday through Friday work schedule. That he had all the comforts of an air conditioned office. While the entertainer, street fenders, food service worker and basic cleaning had a totally different reality.

"Reuben, forgive me but if you don't like your job, do something about it. If your embarrassed by what you do for a living, go back to school."

"Danny, fuck you, I have always been proud of what I do, and I will continue to sing long after your computers have replaced you ass."

"Please, tell me what the hell I did Reuben?"

"The hell if I know. I've had a dozen fellow singers ask me if I need back up singer when I do my impression of Marilyn Monroe singing happy birthday in a falsetto for my boyfriend at one of the local clubs tonight? Is that your way of showing me off as your hot property?"

"Damn it Reuben, I was just joking when I told some of the other guys down in the tunnel."

"Were you also joking when you told all the queer tunnel rats that your loose- assed house boy was gonna make you sing all night long?"

It goes without saying the car ride into work was ever so silent and very cold for central Florida. Just before getting out of the car, Rueben let Danny know if he wanted the relationship to continue, he best be at the employee parking lot on time, and when they got home it better shine like the top of the Chrysler building, or there would be hell to pay.

As Reuben walked into the costume department to pick up his uniform for the morning shows, he couldn't help but to think of his life after leaving New York City.

He stuck to the instructions given him by the U.S. Marshals and never once looked back. Funny how the last two years somehow just flew by.

Even funnier was what Reuben first thought of the move down south as being some sort of punishment for something he had done. If anything, the last two years taught him that for some people, life is about family members and the employment is just a means of support. While others think of their work as what gives them satisfaction, with friends and family being a secondary concern. The latter of the two was the case for the boy from midtown Manhattan. As Reuben's heart began to harden. He told himself the only thing he missed was his mother, and a three hundred foot tall lady out in the harbor.

TWELVE

Kathy, in her heart of hearts, thought it was best if her boss and friend knew all of her options.

"You do know that in the State of Virginia, you can let an employee go for any reason at all!"

"What are you talking about?"

"Cindy, please tell me you know the termination laws here in the Commonwealth."

"Well Kathy, I'll tell ya this. I have no idea what you're talking about, and why would I? Who are we letting go?"

As the ladies continued with the lunchtime conversation, it became all the more evident. One wanted heads to roll, while the other wanted to forgive and forget. As Kathy continued to state her case for letting both of the employees in question go, Cindy played devil's advocate. Kathy reminded Cindy of the reasons for having a non-compete contract. She also went on to ask if a letter of termination should be drawn up for either one, if not both.

"Cindy it's just bad business to keep them both on the payroll."

"Is it really, good business that is? So we fire one, if not both of them, then we sweep it under the rug and see what happens in say a year or two. And what if something like this happens again? Would you prefer we set a standard of no fraternization? If we do, then next thing you know it starts to feel less family and more corporate around here."

"Cindy, this place is your father-in-law's legacy! What they did was wrong! Then there's poor Mrs. Mancini."

"Yeah, not something a married woman wants to go through, that's for sure. Kathy, what we need to do is walk the walk and not just talk the talk! We need to do right by both of them."

"I'm sorry Cindy, but what are you talking about?"

"I love ya my dear friend, but I feel a new Bible teaching coming up in the woman's Sunday school class. Do you not remember? Jesus taught us to love one another as he loved us. I think that alone should settle your heart. Also, remember; never take revenge into your own hands. Leave that to the righteous anger of God. Actually, I'll tell ya what you really need to concern yourself with."

"Yeah, what's that Cindy?"

"Who's gonna do the lawn-mowing this season? I just found out the young man down the street moved away. He was excepted at UVA!"

# # #

With both the Suzuki boys spending most of the summer as camp counselors, someone was needed to help out at the restaurant over the summer.

"Nic, I am glad to see you got all your paperwork filled out for reporting your taxes. I'm gonna get Mei to show you around the dining room, as well as the kitchen. She will show you all of your side work, you know, all your duties, before you leave at the end of your workday. You will be okay waiting on tables only if you listen well to your teacher."

"Working in the dining room is easier than working back in the kitchen trying to make sushi or dumplings and such. Nic, for all my years running a kitchen, my mother still tells me I don't make a good dumpling."

"Mr. Suzuki, I just want to say thanks for letting me try and fill in for Yoshi while he and his brother are at camp. I really do need to earn the extra money right now."

"Nic, work has never hurt anyone; it is a good thing. Like I said, Mei will teach you everything you need to know, so listen well!"

As the conversation between Mei and Nic started, she told him that the hardest thing is learning to fold the napkins.

"You know it's the napkin origami."

"But Mei, you make it look so easy."

"Silly boy, I've been doing this since I was five or six years old. Nic, if you can test out of Mr. Albert's advance placement trigonometry, you can fold a napkin."

The more time Nic stood there watching Mei, the more he became all the more lost in what some might have called puppy love. However he made a go at being witty and charming like his older brother.

"I don't know, I've been doing trig since I was like nine or ten, you know."

"Yoshi says your sense of humor is hard to follow, but I think you're very, very funny. Are you cold or something, I see that your hands are shaking?"

"Yeah, that's it. We only have one air conditioning unit at the house, and it's upstairs. So no, I'm not used to this ice cold air."

"Not to worry. On a Friday or Saturday night, when the dining room is full, it stays rather hot in here."

As the morning progressed, Nic learned first-hand how much of a passion Mei had for history. He thought to himself, if she liked it, there was no reason for him not to. Mei talked about the similarities between the Japanese and the Italian people during the internment just after the start of World War II. She spoke on how both Jews and Buddhists had learned the importance of listening to their elders. She soon reminded Nic of the similarities the two of them shared; how both his mother, and her father, grew up working with food.

"You will need to know how soy, vinegar, wasabi, and ginger will affect the flavors of the meal."

She also let Nic know just how important napkin and silverware placement was to her father. She continued to give instructions on everything, including how to pour the water so as not to spill it. Soon enough, her lessons on serving and removing plates and the other things a good waiter needs to know, became nothing more than a humming noise in the back of his head. Nic found he was unable to comprehend anything she said, and he just stood there and drank in the beauty of his first crush.

She turned to ask him a question, only to see him become befuddled, then blush with embarrassment. Mei was quick to turn and cover her mouth with her hands in order to stifle a laugh, and to help Nic save face.

Later that afternoon, Yori found his young friend looking at his daughter and asked him if he liked what he was looking at? Nic responded with a most enthusiastic "Yes!" Mr. Suzuki politely reminded him that he was Mei's father. At that, Nic simply dropped his head and turned to walk away.

Hachi asked of her husband, "So do you think he'll make it?"

"He won't be with us forever, but he'll make it through the summer, if he can get over his infatuation with our daughter. Oy Vey!"

"Yori, I don't think you used that correctly!"

"Yeah, I did."

# # #

Thinking they might sill have a chance to work things out, Reuben gladly accepted Danny's invitation to lunch. Sadly enough, Danny had made a few decisions about his carrier as well as a few other things.

"Hey guys, you do know that as employees of the park you get an even larger discount, if you make the meal to go."

"Thanks, but we're here for the ambience!"

"We're here for the ambience? Come on Danny you are kidding, right? I could think of a dozen other places here in Orlando, and you want to come on property. You seem like your a million miles away this morning, what gives?"

"Well, here's the truth Rueben. You see I've been a bit deceptive. Yes, I brought you here because I know you need this job, and you also enjoy working here."

"What are you trying to get to?"

"It's simple, you're smart enough to know you don't turn out a place where you work. What I mean by that is, I could take you anywhere else, and you would more than likely go crazy! Here, you will clench your fist and grit your teeth, but you will do so with a smile on your face. Because you need to keep you're cool, and give me yet another award-winning performance. And the Oscar goes to Reuben, if that really is your name. Keep breathing, in, out, you're doing very good."

Danny continued without even taking a breath. "Two and a half years ago when we first met, I just knew you were out of my league. Hell, who are we kidding; a geek like me with a pretty boy like you.

The night I met you, you made my heart skip a beat, but back to why we're here today. Damn it, the fact is that you and I are going nowhere fast. You're so good for my ego, but you're killing me. I want more, no, I need more. You have built a brick wall around your heart, and if I start chipping away right now, I'd be dead and in the grave before finding it. You do know you talk in your sleep, don't you? Hell I've been listening to you at night while you call out for him. God knows I wish I were your Andy. He must have been something else!"

As Danny continued speaking, Reuben only thought was just how much information had he let slip out.

"Reuben, I'm not as stupid or emotionally inept as you might believe. It would have been nice to know that all you wanted was a fuck buddy to provide you with stud service. I've never known you to have any kind of past, I do hope that wasn't your Andy you lost last year with the Olympics tragedy. Sadly, my friend, I have chosen not to renew any of my contracts. Digital Animation Systems Control offered me a ton of money to stay on with them. I was offered a job down in Houston, and we'll, my family is up in Fort Worth, so I think it will be a good thing for me to move back to Texas."

"Well, shit and be damned, is that really how you feel? Wow, I assume you're in the process of breaking up 'cause this doesn't sound like you're asking me to go with you, that's for damn sure. Man, I so wish I was shitfaced; this might be a little easier to take!"

"As difficult as this may sound Reuben, I had to do it this way, otherwise I would have ended up staying. My next boy friend can be as plain Jane as I am, just so long as I can get close to his heart. I was so close to begging you to come with me to Texas. But I know it will never change with you."

"Well hell, get along little horsey. Yippee, yi, yo, kayah! I can be more open, really I can. Why didn't you ask me to come with you? Why are you leaving? I thought you loved your job, and I thought you loved me."

"I swear, I thought you were just a singer, but I now see you're an actor also. That little performance was worthy of an Emmy, or was it an Oscar."

"Is it to late for some honesty now? Actually, it's The Antoinette Perry Award for Excellence in Theatre, and I was once nominated. I didn't win, but that's life.

Well, let me correct that last statement. I wasn't nominated; the person I use to be was, but that's a long story, and I'm not allowed to go into it. Hell, if I thought for one second it would keep you here, I would tell you. I would tell you all about my five cousins, my two aunts, and my one uncle who died last year in Germany."

As the tables themselves had been turned, Daniel Miller sat with a puzzled look on his face. Reuben did have a past, but Daniel wondered why he had not been privy to it.

"Hell, I'd tell you about my kid brother; God knows I love and miss him. I love my mom, and I truly miss her; hell, I even miss my dad. And yeah, let's not forget my ex, Andy. Just to put you at ease, you two are nothing alike! But here's the thing. I can't say a thing, because with every detail I tell, I put them all at risk. My coming down here was supposed to keep people from getting hurt. I'm sorry for screwing with your head and your heart. Shit, where's that glass of vino bianco? I just didn't think that with you being a freak of a genius you would be so passionate and interested in all the details. Who are we kidding? I just hoped it would be breakfast, dinner and sex, and that you would be happy enough to never ask me anything. Never mind. I gotta get the hell out of here!"

THIRTEEN

Albert Einstein is most often quoted as having said, "The definition of insanity is to do the same thing, yet expecting a different result." Annie had had enough to know she needed to go outside the salon to find her next receptionist. She also knew she may have to let a few others go as well.

"Nicky, I'm not in the mood to be questioned by you like that, do you hear me? I told you, I don't know what she wants!"

"Mom, why would one of your best friends want to talk with me?"

"I don't know. If nothing else, just give her a ring. The number's MAJ-1414, and be polite to her, you hear me boy?"

"Good afternoon, may I please speak to Mrs. Annie? Oh, this is Nic Mancini."

"Hi Nic, it's Annie. I'm a little crazy right now. I have a few fires that need to be put out, but please if you can, meet me at Eggs 'n' Things in about two hours."

"Sure, but do you need me to call the fire department?"

"No, not that kind of fire, but thanks for offering."

"Okay, I'll see ya then."

Nic had never been to Eggs 'n' Things, nor could he ever remember being in any kind of greasy spoon diner, but he'd heard that they tended to be very loud and busy. Eggs n' Things was not at all what he thought it was going to be, when he arrived it was calm and quiet. Just about the time his cola showed up, so did Annie.

"Hello Miss Annie, I hope you are doing okay. Over the phone you sounded like your day was a little crazy."

"Young man, crazy would have been nice, believe me."

"Miss Annie, can I get you a coke or something to drink?"

"Yes, but I don't think Eggs 'n' Things has a happy hour. No Nic, in all honesty, I am heading over to Dan's Hideaway, after you and I finish talking. If you were old enough, I would invite you to go with me. I do need to ask you something."

"Okay Mrs. Annie, what's your question?"

"Your mom and I are good friends and I understand where she is financially. She has two mouths to feed, and sooner or later, rent to pay. She needs to work the floor at the shop and build a clientele to bring in some real money. I understand you have about a year and a half 'till you can touch your trust fund for college."

"I see my mom has told you everything."

"Well, not everything, but enough that you might be the person I truly need."

"Mrs. Annie, what do you mean?"

"Well the shit hit the fan today and, oh, forgive my French; I'm sorry."

"It's okay, my dad says the word shit all the time, some times he'll say fuck it or damn it as well."

"We'll that's nice to know, but at any rate it hit the fan this morning, and starting Tuesday, I need a new receptionist who can also manage the shop, and who won't try to rob me blind. I just caught Medusa my bookkeeper with her sticky little fingers in the cookie jar, along with her sisters the Gray hags of Greek mythology trying to put the screws to me."

"Why me, Mrs. Annie?"

"Well, that's simple. I need brains to do the books, charm to answer the telephone, as well as good looks at the front door. I know you have all three. You have the time, and you need the money."

"Well, it sounds like you have it all worked out."

"Not at all. I want your mom to come and work with me when she graduates from beauty school. I also don't want to have to replace you in seven or eight weeks after I've gotten you broken in. The plan is for both you and your mother to let me know one way or the other. Will you talk with her about it and then meet me here again tomorrow?"

"After I talk to my mom what time do you want me here?"

"Nicky, you tell me."

"How about 10:00 am?"

#

If there is any truth to the saying, "Hell hath no furry like a woman scorned," just try to piss off a gay man and live to tell about it. Danny was just about to receive a life lesson.

"Reuben, where the hell have you been all day?"

"I don't see where that is any of your damned business, at least not anymore!"

"Come on, I was just concerned about you."

"To hell with you Danny, and your concerns."

"Reuben, I was hoping that regardless of what happens between us, we could remain friends."

"Friends? What the hell is wrong with you? Friends lend you a shoulder to cry on when you don't make the cut in a cattle call. Friends go with you to see a bad movie. Friends let you drink all their wine or smoke all the pot in the house; that would be a friend. We lay together in the same bed for two and a half years, and now you just want to be friends? I say to hell with you, Danny Miller."

Danny who had just started on his second cocktail of the evening suddenly felt the need to guzzle what remained of it.

"You want to know where I've been all day? Shit, I'll be happy to tell you. I went over to a friend's place, we smoked several bowls of his weed, and then before I knew it, I was in the kitchen cooking dinner from an old family recipe.

I've been told I make a fabulous Alfredo sauce, but apparently I don't make such a good lover. I spent the day with a friend, but I didn't have sex with him today.

So let me ask, where the hell have you been? I bet you've been out interviewing your next boyfriend. Oh that's right, you already have one don't you? Make sure he has a past. Don't forget to ask him why he ran away from his parents' home in Hawaii, or how old he was when he moved five thousand miles east to live in New York City because he couldn't hide who he was anymore."

"Reuben, what the hell are you talking about, a new boyfriend?"

"Danny Miller, are you not the most anal retentive person on this earth? You need for everything to have a place, and your always preaching that everything shall remain there. Can you tell me why things are suddenly out of place?

Have you forgotten I do the laundry? As gross as it is, I found a pair of your tighty whities with a bloody skid mark. So just how endowed is your new boyfriend? So, let me ask, does he even know you plan on leaving?

Let me ask, when does all my junk need to be out of here? Danny boy, don't you lose a minute's sleep worrying about this pretty boy. Momma didn't raise no fool. I put almost every paycheck in the bank, and guess what? After two and a half years, I'll be just dandy. And by the way, I am still out of your league! Here's a lesson for you. Not all pretty boys are stuck on themselves. I do like my men to have a few extra pounds, a brain, and a personality. If only you had spoken to me, let me know there was a problem. I guess that's just water under the bridge. As for names, hell will freeze over before I ever tell you my real one!"

#

As Annie saw Nic walking towards the salon, she dropped her cigarette to the ground then stepped on its butt while adding a twisting motion with her foot. She then stood up from where she had been leaning against the front door of the salon.

"Nic, I must admit, I am so glad you showed up, and that you said 10 a.m. I was afraid you were going to be one of those early birds." No sooner had she finished what she was saying than Nic looked at her with a devilish grin, and told her, "To tell the truth, I am, but I figured with it being a Sunday morning, I'd give you a break."

"Nic, please tell me I haven't just opened Pandora's box."

"Whose box?"

"If you're ready to get started with your new job. The first thing you need to learn is the menu to Eggs 'n' Things. The crew and clients love that place. You'll be spending a wee bit of time over there. If I remember correctly, it's no dairy and meat on the same plate, right?"

"That would be correct, if you are feeding my mom. I'm not that Jewish. To tell you the truth, I don't know what I am right now."

"Well then, let's make little pigs of ourselves, and the pun truly was intended!"

"Good one, Mrs. Annie."

As they walked in, the wonderful smell of waffles greeted them both. Followed only by bacon and some slightly burnt toast. As the two of them sat down on the red padded vinyl-covered stools, Annie set the tone by letting Nic know a thing or two.

"By the way, from now on it's just Annie, got it? Now let's eat."

"Okay, if it's going to be Annie, I must tell you right now. My mother is the only one who gets away with calling me Nicky; I'm begging you, from now on it's Nic.

"I guess I can handle that one! I wanted your mother's approval. I assume she said yes. I want to keep your mom as a friend! As a businesswoman, your mom can make money for me. You will cost me, and no one knows it better than me. It takes money to make money! Are you ready to get to the beauty shop?"

"Wow Annie, I must admit I never knew it was this quiet on Colley Avenue in the morning."

"Monday through Friday it's not. However, Saturday afternoon till Monday morning, it's like a ghost town around here." As Nic and Annie walked back towards the salon, she extended a hand to wave at her brother Tom as he walked into the church across the street. Nic started to apologize as he realized the time and day of the week.

"Nic, don't apologize. I love my brother and his preaching, but he hasn't said anything new in years. Aside from that, I'm not the best Christian on the planet. You know something, Nic, we might work out to be each other's salvation!

"Let me tell you a nice little story. Your mom and I are more alike than you may have ever realized. We both have a brother and sister and we both are the middle child. Also, we both have suffered tragic losses. I was once married, and even had a child."

"Had? What happened to them?"

" It was game five of the World Series, and the Yankees were up 5 to 3 over the Giants at Yankee Stadium. That day New York won the series, but I lost my world."

"You know Mrs. Annie, you don't have to tell me anything you don't want to."

"Nicky, what did we say, it's Annie and Nic, right? And I know I don't have to say anything. It was Wednesday, October 10, 1962. My God what a day that was. That afternoon there was something on the radio about an accident on the Lexington Avenue Line. It wasn't till the sun started to set that I thought about the fact that my husband and son hadn't made it home from the game. Then, two of New York's finest showed up at my front door. As for the loss of family members, like your Uncle Jacob, or your brother Tony, I think I understand somewhat. My sister Betty hasn't always been so gruff, you know. I think she simply grieved so much for my loss, she had a mild stroke about six months after Robert and Bobby died."

"I really did try to take care of everything, but before I knew what happened, I took a dive headfirst into a bottle of Old Hennessy's cognac. My brother Tommy was on a sabbatical somewhere in the Scandinavian countryside, when he got called home to take care of his two old-maid sisters."

"Wow, that explains why you two hit it off so quickly, but I gotta ask, what's an old maid?"

"Oh God, it's going to be such fun to have you working here!"

"Annie, why do you say that?"

"Well, truth is, there's nothing more jaded than an old hairdresser. It's gonna be fun to have some young blood to laugh at, and with."

"Thanks a lot, but tell me the rest of the story."

"It was the Christmas of 1965 and I was in the middle of Herald Square, when out of the blue my world fell apart. It hit me that Robert and I were never gonna grow old together, much less retire down South and make fun of all the southerners and their silly ways.

I was never gonna dance the mother and son dance with Bobby at his wedding. God, I miss him so much and sometimes I think I see him, or what he might have grown up to look like. Christmas is for family, but New Year's is for friends. On Christmas Eve morning, my heart wouldn't allow me to see either one. I went out to the local bodega, stocked up and, well..."

"Annie, come on. Don't stop now! Continue telling me the story! How did ya get from Midtown in the winter of 1965 to Ghent in the fall of 1973?"

"That night Betty and I had a nice dinner, exchanged our gifts with each other, and watched some television together. After she went to bed, I walked out on the balcony and started working on the Hennessy. I assume you know nothing about cognac and how it makes you feel so warm and toasty. I'm here to tell ya that it doesn't take long for a fifth of cognac to knock your socks off, and probably your coat as well. I was completely out of it, but the next morning Betty found me. When I woke up, I was tethered to a bed in the hospital, and labeled as an attempted suicide. Next thing I know, Tommy came to save his two sisters and put in for a church anywhere south of Washington, D.C. A few weeks later, I ended up here, telling my story to the owner."

"Several months later I'm down at Miss Margaret's beauty school, learning a new skill and attempting to forget some of the past. It's hard to believe it's already been eight years; life is crazy. That's for sure."

"Annie, let's be truthful with each other. If you're looking for a bookkeeper, that's fine, but I really don't know anything about your industry, nothing, not a thing."

"Nic, the question isn't what do you know, it's more like are you willing to learn so you can earn the money you and your mom need for the time being? Once you start college, all bets are off. I'll start looking for someone new. I might just give the salon to your mom and let her have some fun with it."

FOURTEEN

"Delilah," Annie said, "If I could get you to understand anything, it would be that beauty school is nothing more than a means to an end. Be the first one there in the morning and the last one out in the evening. Unless you're dying, never miss a day. Before you know it, you'll be out making money for yourself, and not for the school."

Delilah poured herself into the school so much, that when the day came that she and her fellow students were set free on all the people who were crazy enough to become beauty school guinea pigs, she could barely contain herself. Delilah's favorite teacher let her and everyone else know that on Tuesday when they returned, they would be part of the senior class. And they would be assigned a locker, and a workstation. They would still have to attend the regular hour and a half of theory class. She also reminded them that Tuesday through Friday would still require them to wear their uniforms.

"On Saturdays you can dress like you're working in a modern salon. Also, don't be nervous, but you'll get your first live clients starting next week."

You could call it whatever you wanted to, a jinx, a curse, or maybe even pride, but at the end of the week, when everybody else was talking about how badly they had cut themselves or their customers, Delilah boasted she hadn't cut anything. Just a minute or two later, as she was called up to the desk to give a haircut, she learned to never again boast about anything.

As she said "hello" to her next client, fear overtook her. The woman was the smallest Asian woman she'd ever seen. In the back of her mind all she could hear was, Asian hair has the thickest cuticle layers of any hair type. It's the hardest of all hair types to cut. It also shows every mistake." If she had ever heard anything negative about Asian hair, it came rushing back to her at that moment.

When she was done, she, her instructor, and the client, all agreed the cut was very good. With the enemy of good being better, Delilah thought she saw the smallest bit of hair that needed to be snipped. As fate would have it, in an attempt to make the nice cut even better, she went back in to make that final cut.

The dry hair seemed thicker than it ought to be, so as she applied the slightest bit more pressure to the shears, the client let out both a scream and a high flying squirt of blood, which ended up on the lady seated next to her.

As the client left that afternoon she told Delilah, "One day people will wait in line to get into your styling chair; however, I won't be one of them."

#

From time to time, Annie required her staff to come in for a mandatory Monday morning meeting. Truth be told, she jokingly called it nothing more than her witchy bitchy sessions. With only ten minutes till the start of the meeting, the beauty salon looked, smelled, and sounded more like a Saturday morning at full capacity. There was a haze from cigarette smoke and the sound of a dozen women chit chatting, along with the smell brought about because several of the older operators never forgot to bring their flasks of alcohol. When clients are around, the average hairdresser might act demure, prim, and proper. However, when the client is out of sight, it was 'no holds barred.' Annie knew how to keep the natives from getting too restless. She made sure there were plenty of donuts and coffee, as well as soda pop, to be used as a mixer.

"Okay, it's the first week of November, and a few of you old-timers know what that means. Not only is it time to do the pre-holiday clean, but its high time we all sat down and had ourselves a nice little chat."

For the three new employees at Shear Delights, it was the chance to get up on a soapbox and bitch and bellyache, if they had the nerve.

However it would seem that today's meeting was not necessarily an open mic night, as Annie had a long list of grievances.

"As some of you know, two of the old timers were given their walking papers a few months ago. Now, I've heard a nasty rumor that some others want to join them. If that is the case, I have boxes in the back room just waiting for you to put your shit in and go! Let's talk about numbers, a subject most of you usually cringe at. I got here eight years ago and joined a rag tag team, and thought nothing of it. Five years later, Sally Ann asked me to step into her role as the ringleader. I still question if I made the right choice. The question now becomes, can the doors of this fine establishment remain open, even if two of the three originals departed for another shop? Hell, at this point I'll go so far as to say, 'Without a doubt, yes we can!'"

As all good salon owners know, you simply can't keep a hairdresser's attention any longer than half an hour. It was by sheer force of will that she kept the questions at bay long enough to explain all the changes that were coming.

Laura Walker, one of Annie's long-time clients, worked out a bartering deal. Her husband owned a very high-end lumberyard with only the finest of wood available. It turns out there was a major purchasing mistake that worked to the advantage of Shear Delights.

Annie's happiest moment came when she told everyone that the 1950s Vintage white French provincial décor was on its way out the door! Moments later, she explained that in order to allow the workers every minute they needed, a change in shop hours was coming. They would be closing earlier on Saturday, along with opening later on Tuesday. They cheered at the news, and she called the meeting to an end.

"Nic, do me a favor if you will. Stick around, because I bet you dollars to donuts the 'grays' are going to try to bury me in questions, and I will need a way out, okay."

"Okay with me boss, but why do you call them the 'grays'?"

Annie laughed, and quickly explained that in Greek Mythology there were three girls who were born old and gray, they shared one eye and a tooth between them. They were forever fighting over everything, including the eye and tooth.

They were called 'The Grays' simply because of their appearance. But what really made Annie laugh the most, was that the sisters were simply known as Horror, Dread, and Alarm.

#

When the remodeling of Shear Delights started to run into the pre-Christmas crunch, everyone became a little concerned. Annie told them to tell all of their clients it was her fault for the holiday mess. It was an unwritten rule that salons were always closed on Sundays and Mondays. With Christmas falling on a Tuesday this year, Annie chose to have the big party on Saturday, and would keep the shop closed till the following Thursday. Over the years, anyone who thought himself or herself part of the who's who in Ghent was always at the Shear Delights Christmas Eve party.

It was the place to be for hors d'oeuvre, along with the best cakes, candies, and endless bottles of wine. Delilah and her fellow Jewish friends knew it was not kosher wine, but then, what about Christmas was kosher? No, it was just a time for all the local women to come exchange gifts with each other. This time of year at the beauty shop had very little to do with faith, and everything to do with sisterhood.

Annie wasn't alone in giving end-of-year bonuses. Most if not all the employee's clients made it in that Saturday to remind their stylist of their devotion by way of a yearly tip. Most of them walked in with a big gift and an envelope. The customers tried to outdo each other with the size of the gift. Most of the employees were more concerned with the contents of the envelope, for they all knew what was inside that envelope, and it would help keep body and soul together through the roughest month in the hairdresser's year, January.

Several days later as Betty and her brother were setting up for the special Christmas Eve service. Nic who had grown so fond of his boss, and had turned into the truest of mensch, begged his mom for some help. He wanted to help his favorite goy through what was supposed to be a wonderful night. He knew that with her loss of husband and child, Annie simply wished the saddest night of the year would simply go away.

As Annie walked into the Mancinis' home she was surprised to find a small Christmas tree along with a stocking hanging near the fireplace. As Delilah put Suzie down for her long winter's nap, Nic joked about the fact they were going to confuse old Saint Nick!

FIFTEEN

As far back as Nic could remember his father had always had a party of some sort to attend on New Year's Eve. That's why Nic was shocked to see Rico walking throughout the house at 8 p.m. with no signs of his tailor fitted tuxedo.

"Dad, what's going on? I thought you'd already be on your way out to somebody's party by now?"

"Nic, I think Lucy and I are going to stay right here this year."

"Shit, you're going to do what?"

"That's right my son, we are going to stay put for the night. I'm telling you, you won't even know we're here, quiet as church mice. We'll stay out of your way."

At that, Nic wanted to cuss his father out. He also knew he had no choice in the matter. He would have to simply bit his lip, but that was easer said than done.

"Nic, we just want to get to know all your friends and co-workers, that's all."

It was with Rico's statement Nic lost all control of his tongue.

"Dad, cut the crap, I'm not sure what's going on, but don't all your co-workers go over to her place every year? Why the change in venue, do your co-workers know just how toxic you two really are? Also, why would you want to be at your ex-wife's New Year's Eve party? Don't tell me now that you caught your fuckie suckie, five buckie bitch, there's no more fun in chasing her?"

"Ouch Nic, that one hurt. I must hand it to you, that was a great attempt to provoke me into showing my ass, for all your mother's friends."

"Dad, you don't have to show your ass, everybody coming over tonight already knows you are an ass. Besides that, I'm sure you'll be bored because you won't be the life of the party."

It wasn't even 9 p.m. and the kitchen was packed with food. Delilah, Hachi, and Samantha had spent several hours earlier that afternoon getting everything prepped before rushing home to get dressed up for the last party of the year and the first party of 1974.

Nic thanked Dan for loaning him all the glasses from his bar, and for donating the mixers and ice. Nic, in true Mancini style, played host, with more charisma than anyone could have expected from such a young man. Nic told several of the guests how it seemed funny that he wasn't old enough to drink, yet he was host and bartender.

The surprise of the evening wasn't the amount of salon clients who showed up, it was the fact that 'the gray sisters' graced everyone with their presence, and seemed to have a good time. Mei, Yoshi and Nic found themselves in the kitchen going through a crash course on opening champagne bottles. From 11:30 on, filling the champagne glasses became their only job. It was a typical New Year's Eve party, with sounds of Auld Lang Syne and shouts of "Happy New Year". Nic took great pride in the work he'd done and how well the entire evening turned out.

"Mom, I told you I'd do all the cleaning. I'll be there in just a...oh excuse me!"

As Nic rounded the corner into the kitchen he was a bit surprised to find Dan and Annie embraced in what seemed to be the eternal kiss.

"Nic, it was such a wonderful party. Thank you for being such a good host."

"Boss, you're snookered! Go home!"

Annie quickly volunteered her and Dan's services with regards to helping with the cleanup detail.

"Nic, we could stick around to help clean, if you want. I think your mom isn't feeling so good. She looked a little green around the gills earlier tonight. I sent her up to bed about 20 minutes ago."

"No Annie, I'm gonna check on Suzie and my mom, then I'll get back down here and clean everything up. I'll see you on Wednesday morning."

"Dan, now you see why I call him my little right-hand man!"

# # #

The second-largest city on the planet, and the one night the entire world celebrates, Andy and Billy found themselves walking through Hell's Kitchen aiming for Time Square.

"Billy, I can't believe I let you talk me into walking over to watch the ball drop. Are you smoking pot again or what?"

"What are you saying? I'm crazy for being here, tonight of all nights!"

"Well, yeah. What gives?"

"Andy, it's just that I'm missing him. God knows he loved New Year's Eve. Hell, Andy, I thought it might be fun. We haven't been here on New Year's Eve in quite a few years."

"We? You mean you and Tony. Some of us have never been here on New Year's Eve."

"Well then, welcome to America, this is the craziest thing you can do here, other than Mardi Gras in the spring."

"What the hell is that?"

"I thought you prided your self in knowing all things American. Don't worry I'll tell ya all about it at another time."

With some of the coldest winds that year whipping down 46th Street, the guys continued to fight there way southeast. As it had been on more that one occasion, their conversation came around to work.

"So, I hear you're doing cattle calls for a show based on the book 'Chicago' next week. What are you hoping for?"

"Come on Andy, I'm damn near forty five years old. I'll take what ever I can get. Also it's not a real cattle call. My agent got me a reading, so I'm hoping for the best!"

"So Andy, there's a rumor going around that a workshop is getting ready to start up. I also heard only the best of the best dancers are being invited to join."

"Yeah, I got an invite to attend the first meeting."

"Andy I wish you the best, it's a hell of a lot of hard work, with no guarantee that it will pay off in the long run. But I will say, I know you're talented. I hope it works out for you too!"

"Yeah, if it does, who knows, it might lead to my very own Tony Award!"

As the two men came closer to Broadway, they stopped dead in their tracks. They looked at one another and realized there was very little chance of getting any closer to One Times Square.

"Andy, I think we can forget getting any closer to Times Square, let's just find a bar right now and have a toast to him. I miss him so badly. Do you think he is still around?"

"God only knows, Billy. I sure as hell hope so!"

"Hey, barkeep, set up three Bacardi 151s please; and join us if you will."

"Okay guys, thanks much, and what are we drinking to?"

"Here's to our best and long-lost friend, Tony."

They raised their glasses, and Andy gave the toast,

"Tony, if you're still on this planet, we pray we see your face before we leave this life behind!"

After several more shots, Billy asked the bartender, "How much do we owe you?"

"It's New Year's Eve, go, find your friend Tony, and we'll call it even."

# # #

Although he had done it many times before, standing atop one of the parks floats, even with all the safety apparatus, it was not Reuben's idea of fun. Before he had climbed onto the cherry pickers that lifted him up, he carried on a crazy little conversation with one of the many dancers who were performing in tonight's parade.

"Hell, at this point I'd swear to Jesus himself if I thought it would do something to get me off this damned thing and into a fucking bar."

I'm telling you the song has eight lines, and I have to sing it for a half an hour. I tell ya it was my dad's favorite, and nobody sang it better than Guy Lombardi. Hell I say get the old guy up here and let me go."

"What is wrong with these people? It's gonna be 1974 in less than 20 minutes. People get out of here and go to the discotheque, for God's sake."

"So Reuben," asked Larry, Rueben's safety guru. "Whatcha doing after I let you off this crazy contraption?"

"Hell's bells, I'm gonna pretend I'm in Los Angeles and go streaking down Main Street, and if that don't get me fired, I'll get some sleep and come back to work tomorrow afternoon. Why?"

"I thought if nothing else, you could come over, if you want."

"If I ever get out of here, I thought about going over to that new after-hours club. Why don't you two join me?"

"I don't know. My cousin just moved to town and he just broke up with some boy from back home. He's a little down; I think he could use some cheering up. You know, get some of the guys to come over after work. We got plenty to drink, and even more to smoke."

No sooner was the last safety hook attached to Reuben's waist, than the float pulled into place. As the music started, he thought just how lucky he was that at least part of the way through he could pretend to be a cricket, and sing about stars and making wishes.

As he took center-stage in front of the castle, the count down began, after the fireworks finished he sang the one song he despised the most, 'Auld Lang Syne'.

"Thanks for yet another safe trip back down to Terra Firma. Let me ditch my costume, and I'll be ready to go."

"Ready to go?"

"If we're getting that wasted, I'll just sleep on your couch, and get a cab back home tomorrow. By the way, is this some kind of a mercy date? What I mean is, are you bringing me home for him, or is he back there waiting for me? I know, don't flatter myself, right?"

"My goodness, I knew you were full of it, Reuben, but I never knew to what degree."

As Larry and Rueben drove off property and back to the apartment, Larry found himself having to answer a dozen of Reuben's questions.

"Come on, be honest! What's he like?"

"He's a hairdresser. He's good-looking, I mean good-looking enough, better than what's-his-name, that tunnel rat you dated forever."

"Some friend you turned out to be. I told you not to bring him up ever again."

"Here's an idea for ya, he sings off key. We can smoke a bowl and let him be our entertainment for the night."

"That's how you treat your family? I'd hate to see how you treat your friends. Oh, that's right. I'm your only friend. Other than of course that beautiful boyfriend of yours."

SIXTEEN

The life expectancy of a child born with Tay-Sachs is nothing more than two to four years. Sad as it was, Delilah's mother, Deborah Russo, along with her sister Rebekah, knew Suzie's days were somewhat limited. They also knew they were going to spend every birthday they had together as a family.

"Will someone get the door?" yelled Delilah, "My hands are full."

"I got it, Mrs. Mancini."

"Thank you, Mei."

Mei, who simply loved meeting new people, had been eagerly awaiting this moment for several days now. With Mrs. Mancini growing to be almost like a second mom, Mei couldn't wait to meet Delilah's mother and sister.

"Hello, are you Mrs. Mancini's sister and mother?"

"Yes, yes we are."

"We've been expecting you. I'm Mei Suzuki. Mrs. Mancini, your family is here."

"Hi Mom, Becca, it's so good to see you. Mom, this lovely young lady is one of Nic's good friends. Mei, this is my mother, Deborah Russo, and my sister, Becca Zuckermann."

"It's very nice to meet you. Mrs. Mancini, I'll go back and work on the salad, if that is okay."

"Mei, why don't you take a break, and do me a favor? If you will, tell Nic that his grandma and aunt are here."

"Mrs. Mancini, Nic is running around with Yoshi."

"Well, Mom, we may or may not see him for a while. Yoshi is Mei's brother. He and Nic are like Frick and Frack. They live to terrorize the streets of Ghent in Yoshi's old jalopy.

Don't worry though, Yoshi knows better than to be late. The boys will be here just a few minutes before Yoshi and Mei's parents Hachi and Yori arrive."

"Delilah, with all that you've been through this year, it's so good to see you've made yourself some good friends. Now, let's get down to business. Where is the star of today's show?"

After the ladies came back downstairs from visiting with Suzie, all four of them gathered in the kitchen on what felt like the coldest winter's day so far this year. They each found a task to work on before the rest of the guests showed up.

As Mei began to frost the cupcakes, Delilah asked that she leave at least two uncovered. She had been having heartburn lately and thought she would skip the icing. However, when she told her sister to leave some of the pasta without sauce, her mother said that she must be dying.

"Who ever heard of not wanting some tomato sauce on their spaghetti?"

"Mom, I don't know what it is lately, but everything gives me heartburn. I must be going through the big change!"

"Mrs. Mancini, what change is that?" Mei asked.

"Menopause; you'll learn more as you get older."

"Honey, I know I just met you, but my husband Matt is going through that change, and it's not menopause. It's called getting old!"

"Young lady, maybe you'll be lucky. Who knows, maybe Asian food won't cause your husband so much heartburn."

"Mother, don't be telling her stuff like that!"

"It's okay Mrs. Mancini. I don't plan to marry anyone like my dad."

"Well for goodness sake young lady, stay away from Jewish and Italian men. Nothing ever sets well with them."

When the ladies finished their light-hearted chuckles, the doorbell began to ring. The Suzukis showed up first, and this time all five family members were there, including their oldest son who just graduated from college. With the old Japanese custom in mind, Taro had chosen to stick around to celebrate the New Year for as long as possible, hoping his parents would honor the new American custom of allowing him to stay indefinitely and not charge him any rent.

The guest list had grown to include several people who had never met Suzie. Many of them were there after having heard about the mother who was celebrating what could very well be her daughter's last birthday.

Sunday, January 13, 1974 was the day that the Mancini home was packed to the rafters. Many of the ladies from Delilah's beauty school showed up, along with most of Shear Delight's staff, along with a few clients.

As one wave of people settled in, the next wave showed up. Annie and her new beau, Dan, seemed to be attached at the hip.

So, it really was no surprise when they showed up together. The surprise was the number of gifts they had in tow. According to Delilah it, was more than any two-year-old child would ever need.

As if there were not enough guests, four more showed up: Pastor Tom and his sister, Betty, along with Rabbi Benjamin David, who had prayed for the Mancinis after Rico's first stroke. The rabbi brought his fiancée as well. Turns out he was the newest staff member of the temple where Delilah and Nic attended. If this party had taken place on a Friday or Saturday night, no one would have ever believed it was for a birthday, or at least for the birthday of someone so young.

With the party starting at 1:00 sharp, it was now 3:30 and just starting to show signs of waning. Both of the men of the cloth were the first to leave, but not before asking Nic if they could speak with his father.

Nic was truly embarrassed to say that his father wasn't there for his daughter's second birthday. He wanted to tell them both the truth, but decided against it. Rico only came home to shower and change his clothes anymore.

As the clock struck 4 p.m., everyone suddenly departed, leaving Nic with a task he was growing used to, cleaning up after the party. As the dust settled, Nic heard his aunt and grandmother playing with his sister in the living room. He had this sudden urge to know where his mother was. As he entered the up stairs hallway and cracked open her bedroom door, he heard his mother softly humming some show tune she and Tony were forever singing to each other, while rocking back and forth in Suzie's chair. Nic's sense of urgency slowly faded.

# # #

Delilah and many of her fellow students often asked, how is it that you can sit all day long, and the minute you have you station cleaned up and packed away, you get a client? The students hated it when on Tuesday, Wednesday, and Thursday at the very last moment, someone would walk in wanting a haircut. It was only on Friday afternoons, and only if you had about 1,500 hours, did you want to hear your name called out at the end of the day. It was the fourth Friday in March when several ladies were listening very close to the public address system to hear if this week would be the week their names would be called out.

"Ladies, may I please have your attention! Mrs. Debra Thompson with 1,512, Miss Maria Ann Sanchez with 1,509 hours, and Mrs. Delilah Russo Mancini with 1,505 hours, you have all passed the required hours for the Commonwealth of Virginia and the Board of Barbers and Cosmetologists. I ask you to please clean out your lockers. We wish you the very best in your new career paths. Do us proud at your state board exams."

Not even 15 hours later Delilah heard several of the ladies at Shear Delights welcoming her to her new home. Delilah couldn't remember a time when she was so proud of herself. Yet so very terrified of what it was going to be like in the real world working for a living.

Delilah did find herself looking around every once in a while, trying to take it all in. Somehow, she wanted to savor every moment of this day, making the memories last forever.

As the last client was walking out the door, Annie spoke up and said, "Delilah, you did a hell of a good job today! You should be proud of yourself! It's time for you to learn all the crap they don't teach you in beauty school.

Okay ladies, time to pay up; we've all been there before. Delilah, every head you shampooed today is worth 50 cents, and while you are never gonna get rich, we hairdressers take care of our own! You busted your butt today."

In the regular salon, everyone is working to get to Saturday afternoons. Most salons have its version of the end of the workweek party. Most of them taking place in the back room. With Shear Delights, it was across Baldwin Avenue at Dan's Hideaway.

"Delilah, another thing we gotta let you know about. Today, we buy your drinks, but the newbie plays waitress, so get up, and go order the next round."

Instead of Delilah hitting the bar, it would seem as if the bar hit her. Not a split second later she found herself on the floor, questioning what just happened.

"Shit girl, you must be one hell of a lightweight," Samantha yelled out across the barroom.

"What the hell just happened?" yelled Annie.

Delilah Mancini would have never thought that a full day of shampooing and two bang trims could or ever would have caused her any trouble.

"Girl, what is going on with you?" Asked one of the bar's regulars.

Just seconds later Delilah pulled herself up off the floor, turned to her co-workers then asked, "What do you mean? I passed out."

The youngest of the 'Grays,' who had never spoken above a whisper, yelled out to Delilah.

"Hell girl, how many languages do you speak, and suddenly you didn't understand basic English? Your first full Saturday in a real salon, maybe you need to build up your stamina before hanging with us ole-timers."

It's sad to say, but often times our military and their dependents don't always get the best of health care. The diagnoses given the next day by the Corpsman at the Dependent's Clinic was chronic fatigue. With a rather matter-of-fact attitude he stated it was just one of the problems facing older women.

Low iron and a poor diet, along with early stages of menopause. She was told to get plenty of rest and take naps whenever possible. The first time Delilah felt this strange weakness shoot through her was at the New Year's Eve party several months earlier. She felt it again at Suzie's second birthday party, and then again just yesterday at Dan's Hideaway. She made sure to take all the vitamin supplements she could get her hands on. She also napped when possible, but she had no plans on giving up her standing Thursday evening hair appointments, Friday night prayer services at the temple, or dinner at the Suzuki's apartment upstairs on Sunday afternoons.

How on earth had it become Tuesday morning again? Annie knew without giving it a second thought she would walk in to Samantha cleaning her brushes, Nic would be searching the appointment book for mistakes, and Kenny and Sally Ann would be continuing with their on going love hate relationship. They loved each other, but wanted everyone to think it was nothing more then hatred they had for one another.

"So, how was everyone's weekend? I hope you all had a pleasant one. Dan and I went down to the Outer Banks. We stayed at his little bungalow, just down the way from The Jolly Roger. How I love that restaurant."

Kenny was more than happy to divulge every little detail about what he and all his friends did over the course of the weekend. They spent every waking minute at one of the local clubs. He told Sally Ann, that Sunday night's drag show was just the most festive of evenings! A moment or two later, Sally Ann spoke up, and reminded everyone that this coming Sunday was Palm Sunday. While staring at Kenny, she said that she and all the other ladies of the church were getting ready to welcome all the twice-a-year Christians back. This was her annual reminder and invitation to come to church and get right with the Lord. Never mind the fact that Annie's brother was a pastor and worked right across the street.

"Delilah," Sally Ann asked, "Isn't Passover coming up soon? Will you be having to take the whole week off from work?"

"No just the first and last days. Yes, Sally Ann, it starts this year the Saturday before..."

Before Delilah could finish her sentence, Sally Ann went on and on about all that happened that first Easter Sunday after all the Jews killed Jesus. While Sally Ann was driving the point home, Delilah found herself just standing there like a deer in headlights. Sally Ann never once made the connection that maybe her opinion might be offensive to someone else.

Annie grabbed Delilah by the forearm and pulled her into the office then spoke openly.

"Oh my dear friend, all I can do is beg your forgiveness. I forgot to warn you, she is a Zealot when it comes to religion, more than my Tommy could ever be."

"No big deal, a good friend in high school was the same way. She could talk to a wooden Indian about Jesus."

Annie then went on to Delilah that, be it right or wrong, the new kid on the block does most of the grunt work. That she should keep a cleaning rag in your hand at all times. She should also keep an eye out for Samantha. That she was after all, the highest earner and the most talented stylist on staff. Annie went on to say Delilah would be wise to befriend her, and learn everything she could from her, but under no circumstance should she trust her.

"By the way Delilah, I booked you two shampoos and sets for this afternoon. If you want, I'll help you with the consultation, okay? Also, I just needed to let you know, we do have a young man here who works as our receptionist and bookkeeper. His name is Nic, not Nicky. Do you get my drift? You don't want to piss him off. He's very helpful in filling your appointment book if you keep him happy!"

As the day progressed, Delilah learned that each and every one of the employees at Shear Delights had a talent, the only question was, what that talent might have been! Kenny had the talent for undressing each and every male who walked into the salon with his eyes, including poor Nic. Nic seemed to have nerves of steel and the talent to ignore every advance made by the shriveled-up, little old ladies as well as Kenny.

Delilah found that Sally Ann and her sister were blind as bats, as they had a knack for baptizing one another with the shampoo hose. Delilah also learned that those two old broads had everyone beat when it came down to teasing the hell out of hair. As her first real day drew to a close, she watched as each client checked out and rebooked their next visit with Nic. After that each one of the salon operators offered to walk with their clients to their cars.

Samantha looked at Delilah then mentioned that if she would wait she could catch a ride. Remembering what Annie had said, get to know her, just don't trust her, she accepted the ride home.

"Thanks, Samantha, that's very nice of you. I'll have to admit, I am dead dog tired."

Annie yelled from the office, "Girl, you did a hell of a good job today."

"So, where do you live?"

"Over on Graydon, between Colley and Manteo."

"Oh my, you're a local aren't you? I just wanted to take the opportunity to tell you that Annie is truly in your corner. Your station was put between the two of us, so we can help you. We don't want you to be led to slaughter by some of the ones who have been doing this forever. The hair business is slowly coming out of the dark ages, and Tweedledee and Tweedledum are terrified, knowing they are about to be left behind because they aren't willing to keep up. They will tell you I'm greedy and money hungry, but I believe in working smart, not hard. If you've got to kill time, work it to death! I'll see ya tomorrow, right?"

"Yep, I will be there, Samantha. Thank you so much."

SEVENTEEN

Delilah, who was well into the autumn of her life, could tell you the months move quicker than the weeks ever did, and the days simply fly by.

"How on earth did I ever make it this far along?"

"Delilah, I didn't realize that you'd been here a year already. Time sure does fly."

"No, Samantha, I've been here longer than a year now. It's just that I am starting to feel old. Where did the years go? Today is Nic's 17th birthday."

"Delilah, how long you been down here now? You're starting to sound like one of the locals!"

"Oh Samantha, what was that, my English is painful to your ears, and yet it's the Scots and the Irish who leave you close to tears..."

The two ladies broke out singing the next few lines from the show, "My Fair Lady." They both looked at each other and repeated the line.

"You know, there are places where English completely disappeared, in America, they haven't used it for years!"

"Delilah, I swear sometimes it seems as if you and I could be sisters or something."

"Works for me, as long as it's sisters, and not cousins!"

"What do you mean by that?"

"Oh come on, how long have you been in the States? Don't worry about it, it was just that there was this television show about two cousins, one from Scotland and the other from Brooklyn."

"So, are you doing anything with your wee'un?"

"That would be nice, but I'm not even sure if he wants to be around me, we see each other almost every day."

An hour into her day, Annie called Delilah into the office and told her the manager had asked for the afternoon off from work, something about going out to lunch with a friend. Then Delilah was told she would need to man the desk for his lunch break. When she got the chance, she asked Nic about the lunch date. When she got his answer, it was as if she'd been punched in the stomach.

"Oh sorry, Mom, Dad said he wanted to take me out to lunch, and well, I'm gonna try to bury the hatchet. Okay, truth is he said he would let me drive his new Ford Thunderbird. I can't believe he said he would let me drive it all the way out to the oceanfront!"

Nic quickly turned back and told her, "Oh by the way Miss Mancini, as the manager, I just want to let you know your book has been blocked off at 6:00 this evening, something about going to dinner with your son. I hope you two enjoy your night together. I've heard most teenagers don't want anything to do with their parents. It would seem that's not the case with your child."

Funny, but Delilah seemed to float through the remainder of the workday!

# # #

Nic simply sat in the WJDC lunchroom, waiting for his father. As he did, many of the employees who knew of him said hello.

"Good morning young man, it's Nicky right?"

"No it's Nic!"

A few minutes later, a few more people spoke to him.

"Good morning young man, it's Nic, right?"

"Well, at least someone got it right."

"Wow Nic, you're looking more and more like your dad every day. You must be what, 15 now?"

"Seventeen..."

"Nic, is that you? You look like you've grown since the last time I saw you, what was that, last week at your sister's birthday party?"

"That was four and a half months ago."

It wasn't long before someone finally walked through that Nic knew well enough to hold a real conversation with.

"Good morning, Nic, and how are you this nice spring morning?"

"Oh hey, good morning Mr. James, how are you?"

"I'm fine, are you looking for your dad?"

"We'll yeah, but is this report correct?"

"You remember how to read that thing?

"What the Arbitron ratings. Yeah I remember all right."

"Nic, it's sad to say, but your dad had a hard winter. If something don't change, the overnight guy and your dad might be changing spots here shortly."

Before the conversation could go any further Rico walked in the room.

"Nic, my son, are you ready to get going? James, you remember Nic, don't ya, he turns 16 today."

"Seventeen, Dad, seventeen."

"How is it that they keep growing, and you and I don't age a bit?"

"If you say so Rico, but I feel it a little bit more each and everyday."

"Mr. James, it was nice to see you again, please tell your wife hello for me, will ya."

"I most definitely will young man, and again, happy birthday to you."

As is often the case in the South, you never know what kind of Memorial Day you will get. Nic would remember his 17th birthday as being one that was just a bit stormier than he would have liked. As James had said, it was a beautiful spring day. However between Nic and his father you could see the storm clouds beginning to gather.

"Dad, not that I know anything at all about cars, but I've heard the transmission works better when it's put in drive."

"This is true my son, but we're waiting on Lucy, that's all, she'll be out soon." Nic turned to his father, after hearing of her invitation to join them on the father and son luncheon and without the slightest bit of hesitation, he responded.

"You have got to be shitting me. Call me when you cut the damned apron strings. I'll see you the next time you come home to take a shower and change your clothes. My God, you're an asshole."

Nic then jumped out of the car, and so did his father. Rico told Nic to get his ass back in. Nic asked if he should get in the front seat or back seat. He then stopped, turned back to him and made a last attempt at hurting his father the best way he knew how. He let his dad know he had seen the quarterly Arbitron report, and then told him if he got lucky, he could get an overnight shift at the local oldies station.

"But then I question if you really have the talent to make it anywhere else. Dad, I have no doubts that you could very easily take me in a fistfight. Wouldn't that just impress Miss Lucy Chue so much? Dad here's to my last year of having to put up with you and all your bullshit."

Nic was so glad he had taken the time to learn all the shortcuts throughout the neighborhoods, especially the ones that the cars had no access to. While he walked, the tears continued to fall from his eyes. For God's sake, why am I crying he asked himself.

As he walked the nine blocks back home, he thought back on the ups and downs of his short life. There's no doubt Nic loved his mom and dad, but he wondered where it was he could to turn, especially after they had turned on each other. It was easy to understand the stress they both were dealing with, not just the loss of one, but also eventually the loss of a second child.

The more Nic thought about his parents, his sadness turned to anger, as he screamed out to the Lord.

"God, why, why God, why? I'll take care of my mom and sister; you take care of that ass of a father."

After going home and eating by himself, then washing the emotions from his face, Nic walked back over to his place of employment. He spent the rest of his day trying his best to hide all his anger and pain.

"So my wonderful son, where is it you want to go for dinner tonight?"

"I want to go to Uncle Louie's, over at Ward's Corner."

"That's five miles from home, if your going to do a deli, why not go to Hadassah's, right next door?"

"'Cause we eat there everyday. I wanna get out of the neighborhood, and Louie's is so kosher. He'll never show up there. It would be like garlic to a vampire or something."

"Well, let's go pick up Suzie from the sitters and then were off to Uncle Louie's. By the way, what do you mean he'll never show up there? Who's that you're talking about? "

"Mom, I'll let you in on something, this hasn't been the best of birthdays. Mom, here's an idea, let's move into an apartment."

"Okay, where did that come from?"

"He's just such an ass, look at how he treats you. I almost want to say I hate him, no, I do hate him, because of the way he treats you."

"Baby boy, I bet it's more about how he treats all of us. Nicky, things aren't always, as they seem. He could put all three of us out tomorrow, then where would we go? You do know that next year, on your birthday, his child support and my alimony stop."

"How's this mom? Next year on this very night, you, me and Suzie, if she's still with us, will have dinner in our new apartment amongst a ton of moving boxes."

"Nicky that sounds perfect to me."

Then Nic looked at his baby sister and asked, "How about you, Suzie?"

EIGHTEEN

"Delilah," Nic called out, "You're needed in the office, please."

"Annie, you in here?"

"Yeah, come on in and have a seat please."

"Did I do something wrong? I told Miss Johnson if she didn't like it, we could change it. God knows she whines and complains, about everything."

"Yes she does, but that's not what you're in here for. I need to share something with you. You kicked my butt this week. I had Nic total up your numbers for the week. Samantha, as always, was in first place, then you, and then little ole' me. You've been here about a year and a half, and you are in second place!"

It was later that Saturday afternoon that both Kenny and Sally Ann ever so humbly admitted they knew she was the next star stylist at Shear Delights. Then Sally Ann asked if she would be going over to the Hideaway to start the weekend with everybody else.

"Sally Ann, to tell ya the truth, I got nothing going on tonight. Suzie is with one of my girlfriends, and Nic is going out on a date.

Oh shit, I didn't say a word. He doesn't want all you ladies, sorry Kenny, oh, you know what I mean, knowing all his personal stuff. So yeah, I'll be over as soon as I can get my station cleaned up."

Annie never wanted her staff to waste a single moment on anything other than making money or having fun. She insisted that nobody spend an extra minute cleaning on a Saturday. However, Tuesday mornings were the perfect time to clean like crazy. When Delilah finished tidying up, she ran over to Dan's Hideaway, not wanting to miss a bit of the fun.

"Samantha, I thought I was gonna die when you told old Mrs. Williamson that you forgot to put new batteries in your magic wand, and she would just have to deal with the fact that she was never gonna look like Kate Jackson or any of the other angels for that matter."

Samantha had learned over the years that her Scottish brogue allowed her to get away with murder. Her co-workers envied it, but loved it every time she said something that was considered inappropriate.

"Delilah, what I want to know is how the hell you put up with that crazy Miss Johnson. I love how she tells everyone, "Now I'm not judging anyone, but...!""

"Lord knows she's been judging people her entire life!"

"Okay, here's the truth of it all, it's thanks to Annie. She taught me to look at them as nothing more than a dollar bill. On a good day I think of her as Mrs. Franklin, other days she's Mrs. Grant. Today she was nothing more than Mrs. Lincoln, and it took every ounce of strength I had not to tell her to kiss my tokhes."

"Hell, I bet Annie would have let you get away with that one."

It was as everyone's laughter settled down, Delilah burst out, "Someone call my rabbi."

"Why what's wrong?"

"I'm starving, and I'm gonna eat the most non-kosher meal of my life. And frankly, I don't care!"

"If anyone earned them, you did, that's for damn sure."

After everyone had eaten and had a drink or two, someone mentioned the time change and having an extra hour to party with. Delilah, never wanting to be a party pooper, knew she was too pooped to party! She was the first one to grab her bag and run out the door and start heading home. It was as she got halfway there her world changed forever.

As the telephone operator asked, "What was the emergency?" one of the regular diners at Master's Drug store's lunch counter told her.

"I just walked out the door, and this crazy lady was screaming all kinds of obscenities, then she just passed out."

"Where did you say you were at again?"

"Master's Drugs, at the corner of Colley Avenue and Princess Anne Road."

"Thank you, and make sure someone is outside to flag the authorities down."

It seemed like only seconds before the ambulance arrived. The two attendants double-timed it to get to the Jane Doe and get her onto a stretcher and into the ambulance. In a few minutes, they were at the emergency entrance of Norfolk General.

"Get her into room three."

"Okay guys, what do we know about her?"

"Well Doc, the only witness told me all he saw was her spinning around and cussing like a sailor. We do have the two bags she had with her."

"Where did you say she showed up at?"

"Dr. Matthews, she was over at Master's Drugs, right down the street."

"So she's not one of the downtown crazies. She appears to be okay, no cuts or bruising. She's a little thin for a middle-aged woman. Let's get all the standard work ups done, and then call me. Okay boys and girls, welcome to Saturday night."

It was as one of the administrators went through Delilah's bags, they figured out just who their Jane Doe was.

"Doc, our Jane Doe is a Delilah Mancini. I just went through her personal stuff. She's local and lives up the street on Graydon Avenue. I think she has family; she has some photos of some kids and such. That's all we have for now."

As the administrator left, the radiologist was being chased down by Dr. Matthews.

"Well, did we get the results from the CT scan back yet?"

"Sir, it's only been a few hours. What do you think I'm Dr. McCoy, and we're on the spaceship Enterprise? It's only 1975, how fast do you think it should work?"

"Call me when the results come back or when she wakes up."

After her early evening nap, Delilah sat up in the hospital bed and looked around, then got up and looked out into the hallway. Moments later, her physician was called to her room and as he arrived, she was sitting as prim and proper as ever, asking what had happened to her, and how long had she been there.

"Mrs. Mancini, I'm your doctor, Mike Matthew. We've been caring for you since you arrived earlier this evening. I have a lot of questions for you, when you're feeling up to it."

"This evening? What time is it now?"

"It's about 10:30 p.m.; do you know what day it is?"

"Saturday, October 4, 1975; am I right?"

"Yes ma'am, you are. Do you know where you are?"

"In a hospital."

"What's the last thing you remember?"

She went on to explain that she was having a few drinks with some co-workers. She started to walk home the way she had for the past year and a half. She also told the doctor she remembered stepping off the curb at Colley and Princess Anne. Then she woke up on the bed where she was now laying.

"That's good, because that's where you were found."

"I gotta get out of here and find my children!"

"Were your children with you? Mrs. Mancini, we can't make you stay here, but you're not well. If we get someone to take care of the kids, would you stay for the night?"

"I'm as poor as a church mouse and all you doctors cost a lot of money. I've got to go."

"We're a teaching hospital; don't worry about the medical bills. Let's find your kids, then you can answer my questions."

She quickly remembered that Suzie was with Hashi and Nic was out at a friend's party. She ever so sheepishly told Dr. Mathews that her children were in good hands. Next she asked if a car or something had hit her.

"Mrs. Mancini, this is my boss, Dr. Jeffery McDonald, the attending physician for this evening's rounds."

"You don't come across as the cursing sailor type, but we were told before you passed out you were cussing up a blue streak, and you did that again after you arrived here. Forgive us, but is this the norm for you? I also wanted to ask you if you had been sick lately."

"Why do you ask?"

"Well, I just noticed how very thin you seem to be. Most middle aged people tend to put on a few pounds as the years go by."

"I was told by my other doctors it was normal for a lady who is going into menopause to lose some weight. With all the diarrhea and vomiting, it's been hard to keep any weight on!"

"What other doctors?"

"You know, over on Hampton Boulevard, the military dependents' hospital."

"Oh, I got ya."

It was as the attending physician asked Delilah to call him by his first name, Jeff, that he asked if he could do the same; somehow that seemed to be just what she needed. With a somewhat audible sigh, and a grin, Delilah relaxed for the first time in a good many hours.

"Actually Delilah, I was going to say the norm is for most women to gain weight during the start of menopause, not to lose it. Some women start all kinds of odd diets in order to fight the onset of the weight. Are you eating normally?"

"Well, I am Jewish and I try to keep to a kosher diet, but other than that, I'm not sure what you might call normal."

"A kosher diet is very good, and pretty normal to me."

"When you first got here, we ordered a test with a new machine called a CT scanner. It's a wonderful device for seeing right inside the body, like taking an X-ray of the soft tissue parts. The scans will tell us what might be going on inside you. How long has the weight loss been going on?"

"I don't know, about a year."

"Can you tell us if maybe you've been a little depressed or maybe somewhat anxious over that time period?"

"Doc, you just opened up a can of worms with that last question. Let's see. Three and a half years ago my oldest son fell off the face of the earth. Six months later my husband had a minor stroke, and then I find out he is having an affair. Then my daughter was diagnosed with Tay-Sachs disease, and on the same day my brother was killed. Oh yeah, we got a divorce. But hey, I also started my first job ever about a year and a half ago, and other than that, everything's been okey dokey. So yeah, I might be a little stressed!"

# # #

Mathew Zimmerman was caught with his proverbial hand in the cookie jar. He truly was in hopes of getting out of the house before his lovely wife Rebekah found him packing an overnight bag, and heading off to the local airport.

"Who do you think you're fooling? When was the last time you drove more than an hour to meet with a client? Also, what are you doing with all those extra casual clothes in your suitcase?"

"Well, um, you wouldn't believe..."

"Hold that thought, you've been saved by the telephone. Matthew Zuckermann, don't you dare go anywhere, or you too will need an attorney. Do you hear me?"

Becca let out a blood-curdling scream. As quickly as he could, he got to her, Matthew grabbed his wife to keep her from falling to the floor. He pried the phone from her hand and asked who it was. Nic identified himself and said, "She's dead."

"Who's dead?" Matthew asked.

Becca looked back up at Matthew as he continued to ask. She quickly gathered herself together, and demanded the telephone be given back to her.

"Nicky, you did say your sister's dead?"

"Yes."

"Nicky, Nicky, shit. Where's your mother?"

"Upstairs, Aunt Becca. I came down to call on the kitchen phone."

"Nic, you're going to be fine, just fine, do you hear me? Nicky, I need you to listen to me, listen to me very carefully! As soon as you and I hang up from this phone call, I want you to call your Rabbi! You let him know that a family member has passed away and she's still in the house. You let him know your family is on the way down from New York, so the service can't happen today. Also, let him know your aunt and uncle are the only ones you have called. We are the only ones, right?"

"Yes, the only one so far."

"Don't call anyone else. Let your Rabbi do all that. Unlock the front door so he can get in. Are you listening to me?"

"Yes."

"Good, now go through the house and cover all the mirrors. If for any reason, your mother leaves your sister unattended, you go and sit by her side. Do not leave her alone, and do not touch her. Do you hear me? The three of us are on our way down, and we'll be there as quickly as we can. Nicky, we love you!"

Although this turn of events caught him off-guard, he knew enough to keep his mouth shut. He wasn't about to tell Rebekah it was her very own sister he was planning to go and meet with.

"Okay babe, you call your client, reschedule for a week or two down the road from now, and repack your bags. I'll get Mom and my stuff together. Hon, do you think it would be better to leave the car parked at the airport, or take a taxi into the city?"

"Becca, think about this; it's not like we're going to Chicago or Los Angeles. Might it be faster to drive down there? Let me call LaGuardia and see how many flights they have going down there."

"Thank goodness Mom already knew this was going to happen. Matthew, we are so blessed. I just don't understand how Delilah keeps going after all the crap that she's been through. It's like she's a modern day Job."

"Lord knows, I would likely have cursed God by now, and laid down to die."

It wasn't long before Matthew found and booked a flight leaving the city around 7:30, and arriving in Norfolk before 9 p.m.

"Becca, isn't that one of Matt Junior's old suits?"

"Yeah, I'm hoping it might fit Nic. I know he's a bit skinnier than Matt at that age, but he needs something to wear to the service tomorrow."

"He doesn't have a suit of his own?"

"Matthew Zuckermann, are you oblivious to the fact that poor Nicky and Delilah are living hand to mouth? I hate to say it, but if it weren't for Rico, the two of them would be homeless. Even if Nicky had a nice suit, he can't afford for the Rabbi to rend the lapel, much less throw it out in seven days."

Tradition dictates that getting the body into the ground is always the top priority. It was no surprise when, with the first light of day, the Rabbi and several female members of the Sacred Fellowship Society showed up to whisk little Suzie's body away to begin with the purification.

Becca and Delilah stood off to the side as Suzie's body was washed, dried, and placed into the small shroud. Before the slipknot of the shroud was tied off, Becca helped her sister say her final goodbyes. Somehow, Delilah took comfort in knowing her daughter was the only Mancini family member who without a doubt would surely find her way to Father Abraham along with all the other saints in heaven.

"Nicky, we have all been here before. It's an honor to take care of our family members who can't take care of themselves. You have done a great thing by being the Shomer last night and staying with your sister's body. Do you remember Zaide's funeral last year? Your Uncle Jacob, being the closest male family member, had to give the Kaddish. At Jacob's funeral, it fell to your cousin Matt Junior, and today it should fall to your father. If he isn't going to be a responsible family member, it might fall on you at the last moment. I'm going upstairs to help your mom and grandma get dressed. Do you want your Uncle Matthew to come sit with you? I'll send him down. Nic, always remember, we love you!"

As Matthew found his way down the stairs to sit with Nic, he found it his job to become the greeter.

As he opened the door for more and more of the goyim, he found himself explaining the custom of not speaking until after the entire service was over and everyone had made it back to the house. That custom was to show reverence to Suzie. As Matthew began to close the door before the start of the service, he saw a face he hadn't seen in quite a long time. He stepped out onto the front porch and pulled the door closed behind him.

As Rico and Lucy stepped up onto the porch, Matthew asked him to please reconsider entering and disrupting the service. If ever there had been someone Rico joked about not wanting to meet up with in a dark ally, it was Matthew Zuckermann. After Rico did the slightest bit of posturing for Lucy's sake, he turned and left as quickly as he could.

Nic stood next to his sister's wooden casket and spoke lovingly of her, then prayed the Mourner's Kaddish. The entire household found some small sense of peace.

May there be abundant peace for all of us and for all Israel and say, Amen. He who creates peace in His celestial heights, may He create peace for us and for all Israel and say, Amen.

#

It was during their week's stay in Virginia that Becca and Matthew slept in Suzie's room. Delilah's mom, who knew first-hand about the loss of a child, stayed in her daughter's room. It was the morning after the service that both Becca and her mother found they had overslept. As they walked around the house, they found they were the only ones at home. The question soon became where were Delilah, Nic, and Matthew?

"So Johnny, nice office, but where the hell do you have your personal portrait of Dorian Gray hidden? I don't mean to sound strange, but you have not aged a day since the last time I saw you! What's that been, 15 years now? I didn't come down here to tell you how to do your job. Lord knows you're the best when it comes to family law and the occasional divorce. However, as you well know, Delilah is my sister-in-law, and this weighs heavy on her heart. It's the single most important thing she can do to prepare Nic for what is about to happen."

"Mancini? Delilah, I thought you were going to go back to your maiden name!"

"Well, I've had it so long it was just easier to keep it as is. Mr. Westbrook, this is my son Nic. I haven't told him why we're here today. Also, this is a very dear friend and confidant, Miss Annie Stephens. She's the one who will help him through all the things to come."

"Well Mr. Mancini, my name is Jonathan Westbrook. I am an officer of the courts, an attorney, and also a mediator. I have been assured you are quite the intelligent young man. For my own peace of mind, I need to ask you a few questions before we get to the purpose of this meeting. Mr. Mancini, are you familiar with the term 'emancipated minor, or emancipation?'"

"Yes sir, it's Latin, 'ex manus capere', meaning to lawfully set a son or daughter free from parental rules."

"Very good, I am here to help your family do just that. I have been a friend to your uncle Matthew since the dinosaurs walked the earth, but he can only work in the state of New York, otherwise, this would have remained a private family matter. I also want to remind you, anything said in this office stays here and can never be repeated by any officer of the courts. In other words, Matthew and I can never repeat a word of it. Do you understand me?"

"I think so Mr. Westbrook."

"I think so, is not the answer I need to hear, young man. I need to know that yes, you do or no, you don't. Now again I ask, do you understand? What happens here today is very, very important."

"Okay, I do understand you so far, but why do I need to be emancipated? I'll be eighteen in what, seven or eight months? What's going on?"

"Well, it's not so simple. After your father and mother's divorce, and the fact that you and your father are somewhat estranged..."

"That man is not my guardian, my mom is. You should know that, it was part of the divorce settlement."

"Delilah, I truly believe this needs to come from you."

"Nicky, oh dear God, help me through this. Nicky, I need to tell you something. You know how I've lost all this weight, and I'm always vomiting or taking a nap?"

"Yes."

"Well baby, I gotta tell you something."

"Yeah?"

At that precise moment both Annie and Uncle Matthew stepped up and put a hand on each of Nic's shoulders.

"Well, the truth is, Nicky, I, I have several cancerous tumors! I also have a very fast growing cancer; it's called pancreatic cancer. There is no cure, no treatment, maybe someday, but none today.

Baby, I just found out a few weeks ago. I have been to see a lot of doctors, and they all agree, I may not make it to your 18th birthday. Oh God, I love you Nicky, I really do baby."

NINETEEN

"Hello, please just hear me out before you hang up on me! I know this is gonna sound very odd, but is there a six-foot-two, green eyed, 170- maybe 180-pound man who has dark brown hair, and a mole under his left eye living there? Again, hear me out. Here is where it gets odd. Please go and whisper in his ear, 'Lenny,' you are needed on the telephone! Also, find him some paper and a pen as quick as you can, okay?"

"Babe, there's some strange ass woman on the phone who just described you to a tee, and told me to put 'Lenny' on the phone."

At that moment most if not all the color faded from Reuben's face. He almost ran to the phone, and yelled into the receiver.

"Damn it, who the hell is this?"

"Who else calls you Lenny?"

"Maria, how on earth did you find me? Nobody..."

"We don't have the time for all that right now! You need to take down a telephone number. Do you have pen and paper?"

"Hold on, Jimmy, please get me a...good, thanks. Yeah, I got it. What was that? 703- MAJ-1436, room 313, what's the phone number to?"

"Listen to me very closely young man. If it's just your friend and you, fine, but if there are a lot of people there, kick them all out. You won't want to party any more tonight."

"Maria, I haven't talked to you in years, and now you call and play this mystery game with me. Get to the point already! What the hell is going on?"

"Lenny, I'm sorry to be the one to tell you this. Your mother only has hours, not days; do you hear me. Call her right now! Do you understand me? Somehow Nic knew you were still around, and he begged and pleaded with me to find you. He wants her to have some peace before she passes away."

"Passes away, what the hell happened to her? How, what's wrong with her? I gotta get the hell out of here. What's the name of that little town she's been living in? God, I gotta see her!"

"Lenny, damn it, Antonio Lorenzo, listen to me, get it together! Call her, don't you wait another minute. From what I understand, she won't last the night.

Your brother is beside himself with worry that you won't call in time. Any problems you may have with him, you fix at a later date in time. Call your mother."

"Oh my God! Shit, poor Nic, he's with her right now? How is he doing? My God, I swear I can't do this! Let me let you go, will you be at the service? Maria, what about my going to the funeral, is that okay? Oh my Lord, how's my dad doing? Maria? Maria, ya there? Shit, I lost her. Jimmy, my mother is dying, and my baby brother is with her, holding her hand. I swear he's always been the stronger of the two of us!"

For the next few minutes, poor Jimmy paced back and forth, asking what he might do to be of any help.

"Babe, what do I do to help you?"

"Shit, shit, shit, what the hell, Jimmy, I can't believe she's dying."

"Babe, I only want to help, do you need to call her? Do you want me to pour you a drink, hold your hand, leave the room, what?"

"Jimmy, I love you, but I don't think I can steady my hands long enough to do anything. Please will ya pour me a drink, oh dear Lord."?

Jimmy watched, as the man he had grown so very fond of, the man he had fallen in love with, fall apart. He mixed Reuben a drink quickly, but took his time in serving it, as he wanted to eavesdrop on the phone conversation. Reuben asked for an operator assisted call to be placed for a Delilah Mancini. Jimmy's thought was that maybe he had told the truth; maybe he really is Mr. Esposito. It's not that uncommon for a mother to sometimes re-marry. Maybe the new husband didn't adopt Ruben.

Jimmy knew he wasn't going to be sitting at the head of the class any time soon, but it didn't take a rocket scientist to tell that for some reason, Reuben was hesitant about giving his name out loud. And yet he asked for a person-to-person call, which required two names. Moments later, as Reuben rattled off his full name, Jimmy put the rocks glass to his own lips and gulped down its contents. He then quickly remade the drink for "what's his name".

It was as the operator attempted to connect both Tony and Delilah that the only voice Tony could make out was Nic's. The operator asked if both men would speak with one another, and was given a resounding yes!

As soon as Nic said yes, he asked Tony to please stay on the line after he and Delilah's conversation came to an end. It was after he put the receiver next to his mother's head that Nic turned to Annie and fell apart.

"Momma, it's Tony, it's your Broadway baby. No, really Ma, it's me. Momma, I love you...no ma; I'm alive. They made me go away. Ma, I want you to know, I didn't want to go, but it was to keep you guys safe. Momma, I've been living down South the last few years."

Poor Jimmy just stood there and watched as the quiet night he had planned for Reuben and himself disintegrated instantly. He was also shocked to hear the voice of a somewhat talented amusement park singer change to that of a true Broadway star, a star who quickly asked his mother what song she wanted to hear him sing.

As much as Jimmy knew very little, if anything, about musicals, he knew even less about whom Rodgers and Hammerstein were. He, however, had heard of "The King and I."

It was only after hearing Reuben belt out a song about bravery, he heard the slightest bit of a cry in his voice, as he said to his mother, "Ma, I want you to make believe you're brave. Ma, always remember you're as brave as you make believe you are."

It nearly killed him to have to do it, but Jimmy pried the telephone receiver out of Tony's hand and began to ask if anyone was still on the phone.

# # #

No sooner had Jimmy managed to get the local address from Nic, the two men throw some clothes in a bag and jumped into Jimmy's old Volkswagen. Thanks to interstate 95 and a 75 mile per hour speed limit it took next to no time for the guys to get up to Virginia.

"So, let me make sure I get it right, Antonio Lorenzo Reuben Mancini. Now if that ain't a mouth full!"

"Wow, it's been so long since I've heard my real name spoken out loud. Not wanting to sound sappy or trying to make extra points with you, but I'm glad it's you who said it first. Ya know, they didn't really tell you that much. Keep your head down, stay out of trouble, and never, ever tell anyone your real name.

You know, it's crazy, but I would sometimes say it over and over again, when I thought no one was around. They say it helps to keep you and your family members alive.

I've lost two family members while living underground. I don't want to even think of all the other things I've missed with my mom, and fratello, sorry, my baby brother. The conversations we have missed. The stories she would tell me about how pigheaded my dad could be. I used to go and visit with my Bubbe, my grandma, and we would talk for hours. Don't worry, before the week is up you'll be fluent in Yiddish. In all the craziness I forgot to even ask, how much time were you able to get off work?"

"Don't even think about me, you just keep talking. I think you have a few years you need to get off your chest!"

"Did we just pass over the state line? I've only been in Georgia on my way down south. If you want me to drive, I'll be happy to!"

"No babe, wisdom is telling me after those last three drinks, I should just let you talk all the way up to the Virginia border. Thank goodness for Miss Annie and her giving me the directions."

Just as Jimmy and the resurrected Tony Mancini started to walk up the steps the greater was starting to shut the front door.

"Good afternoon, gentlemen you are just in the nick of time, the service is just getting underway. I am so sorry to have to ask you, but you know she was so very popular with so many different people, are you familiar with a Jewish funeral service?

Her only surviving child Nic will be giving the eulogy, and the Kaddish. Please, after he speaks, in respect of her life, we will all remain silent until we leave the graveside and return here to the house."

"We will do whatever it takes to honor her, but please forgive our appearance, we have been driving all night in hopes of getting here in time."

"Well, I must say, you got here just in time. Oh my goodness, man! It's like seeing a ghost. Your friend looks just like a dead ringer for her first son."

After being greeted by the usher at the door, Jimmy and Tony found themselves, like so many others, lining the walls of the living room. With the casket in front of the fireplace, there was little room for the folding chairs that were saved for the ladies of the family. The only exception was Tony's grandpa David Mancini, who was sitting in the front row.

As his eyes looked through the faces in the crowd, there were so few faces he recognized, and then of course, there was Nic, whose appearances hadn't changed all that much.

As the Rabbi took his place and began the service, a change overtook Tony. He felt as if a part of his true character was resurfacing. In Hebrew, Tony started to pray, under his breath, and Jimmy was somewhat surprised.

This was not to be the only surprise that afternoon. With the Rabbi's teaching on the Rending, or the ripping of the outer garment along with teaching of those who are required to mourn. As the family members came forward, Tony was shocked to see it wasn't his Zaide but his father who hadn't aged that well. Bubbe Russo, Aunt Becca, along with Nic, joined him in front of his mother casket. Soon the entire family was in a state of shock as Tony made his way forward. With all the changes to Tony's looks, it was his Aunt Becca who was the first to recognize him. Yet it was his Bubbe who let out the first of many joyous screams.

"Oh my Lord, you have returned my Tony, praise his holy name. Oh my Tony, Lord thank you."

As joyful as most were with the returning of Tony, there seemed to be one person who was unable to deal with the shock of it all. Rico slumped over in his chair and looked up at his lost son and started to slur his words as he repeatedly cried out his name, "Tony, my boy, it's Tony, Tony."

Mr. Westbrook had every intention to honor Delilah by putting all the letters she had given him into the hands of her friends and family, however, with all the commotion going on, he never quite got around to it. He handed the notes to Nic, asking him to make sure they were distributed. As Mr. Westbrook walked out the door he mumbled under his breath, "My God, when it comes to death, these people don't fool around."

"Operator, my name is Rebekah Zimmermann, I am calling to have an ambulance sent to 746 Graydon Avenue. Yes, we have a 45-year-old man here who is having a stroke. Yes ma'am, I'm sure it's a stroke, I think it is his third one. Please hurry!"

TWENTY

Nothing weighs on us so heavily as a secret.
-Jean De La Fontaine

Nic sat, not knowing if his father would survive, then there was his brother. Was Tony going to head back north, maybe back south, and what was to happen to the young man who was with him? Nic grew up with two secrets, one of which was more his brothers than his, the other being he was in a bicycle accident as a small boy and the handle bar ruptured his bladder. From that day, up until about a year ago, he wet the bed every night of his life. In Nic's eyes, those are not the deep, dark, secrets one might think they were. The last several years had managed to put the weight of the world on his back. With his newest secret growing increasingly darker, he hoped his father would die. God knows no one with any worth would miss him, including his Aunt Maria.

The next of the deep and dark secrets was simple; he feared the person he had slowly become over the last few months! True to what his mother had always called him, Dr. Jekyll and Mr. Hyde. He could be a very kind and gentle boy or a most hateful young man.

It was only after reading his mothers letters. He knew he was going to set about manipulating the situation. He knew what he wanted to do had no honor in it. With all he'd been through, he no longer cared. He was about to make a $50,000 windfall for himself. Nic believed he had all the evidence needed to lighten his load, if he chose to, simply by exposing all the deepest darkest family secrets. It would start with his mother's.

Dearest Rico,

What is it some say, with friends like you, who needs an enemy? At any rate, if you're reading this, it means I'm already gone. I am truly glad Nic is old enough to make his own way in this crazy world we live, lived in. I remember Momma always saying, "If he's Jewish, everything will be okay." Believe me, in my letter to her, I'll be letting her know just how wrong she was. She also told me that Pops always said if he were Italian, all would work out. Pops, I'm not so sure if this is what you meant or not.

However, it was the girls in high school who taught me that if you were good in bed, I could grow to love ya, no matter what. So I must admit, of the three lovers in my life, you were very good not the best, but good.

I suspect you have always known I was no virgin on our honeymoon. You, baby, were not my first, nor were you the last. You were not to blame for the Tay-Sachs found in Suzie. Hell, you weren't even her father. I've gone this far, might as well tell you all of it. I know your first child is somewhere in Korea. You see, Rico, Tony is also not yours. Sorry to tell you like this, but thank you for keeping my first child from being bastardized.

You do remember 'Ghost,' from your high school basketball team, super tall, lilywhite guy, from Finland? He was the one I dreamt of being with while we were physical with each other. I had also thought if you didn't return from the war, I was going to find my way back into his arms.

As to who Suzie's father is? Well, let's just say, it was the week we spent in Washington, D.C. with your friend Paco the Taco. You and Taco partied, while I was with the Russians of Rosslyn. Tony's boyfriend Andy was easy on the eyes, but his older brother, no man on this earth could have been any better in the sack than he was.

Rico Mancini, for 27 years I have liked you, and at times, I think I have even loved you!

DeeDee

Dear Momma,

What's left to say, other than this simple reminder, I love you. I always have, and I always will. Mom, all I can say is that I'm sorry to be putting you through this. As a mother who has already lost two of my three babies, I think I know where your heart must be right now. Momma, you have been through more than your fair share. My hope for you is you live long and enjoy watching your six grandchildren, as well as the great-grand baby. Momma, again, I can only say how sorry I am that I am making you bury yet another one of your children. Don't worry, if there is any truth to the saying only the good die young, Becca will be around forever and will be able to take care of you.

Also, forgive me for not telling you myself that I was dying. Telling Nicky absolutely crushed me.

Love always,
DeeDee

Annie,

I knew you and I were going to be the best of girlfriends from that hot Tuesday morning when you and I shared the saltine crackers and the bottle of cheap ass wine in the back room of the beauty shop. I have told you more things than I would have ever dared to tell my mom, sister, husband, or children. I question if this is what Dorothy might have felt like when she said goodbye to the Lion, the Tin Man and the Scarecrow.

It's like saying so long to the best of my girlfriends, Beth, Hachi, and you, but you my friend, are the Scarecrow in my world. Somehow I think I will miss you more than any of the others. No sane woman would ever try, but thanks for keeping an eye out for my Nicky. We know he'll never be your Bobby, but every once in awhile slap the back of his head, and ask if he has lost his mind? Please teach him about living a full life, and what love can really be all about. Teach him about what you and Robert had together. The rest of it he already knows about. If what your brother Tommy and I talked about is true. I know I'll see ya again someday, my friend.

I'm off to see the Great and Powerful Wizard.
DeeDee

Rebekah,

You know how Grams was forever comparing everything to an apple or an orange, well it's true. Ma and you are a true Red Delicious, bright firm and always sweet. Never wanting to speak ill of the dead, but Zaide, Jacob, and I are just like an old orange. We tended to be sour and sometimes even a little spoiled. Sis, I will always love you and as crazy as it may sound, it is because of that love, we chose to do what we did with regards to Nic's future. You, my love, have two children, a husband, a grandbaby and Lord help you, our mother to take care of. You didn't need to take on the extras that come from caring for my crazy teenaged boy. Remind Matthew what he taught me, you can't libel the dead. Tell him to tell you everything that happened that morning in Mr. Westbrook's office. I also wanted to tell you that I was the one who ruined your pink sweater. It happened the night that both Otto Laine and I lost our virginity to each other in the backseat of his dad's car. Sissy, I do love you more than you will ever know.

As Pops would always say it, Becca Boo, I love you, yes, oh yes I do.

DeeDee

Nicky,

My God, where do I even start with you, other than to say you might want to take a seat? I love you more than I have ever loved any other human in my life! There, I said it. Mothers aren't supposed to say stuff like that, but then your siblings aren't here to get upset. My God, I beg you to forgive me, but I've always tried to protect Tony. He got so much extra attention simply because by the time you came along, your dad had already shunned him. That, or he simply knew the truth. The truth is Tony is not your full brother. Between you, me and the fence post, your father has two children, you and an older child who most likely lives in South Korea. Sorry, not sure, but I think it is a boy. Oh Lord, I know this is a lot to take in all at once.

God, is there anything you don't already know? Yes, and this one is going to crush you. You have been through it all with me.

Over the last few weeks, I have set things in motion that I never thought I would ever do. My God, this is what you call a deathbed confession. I have taken two lives. Yes, I placed a pillow over your sister's face and simply snuffed the life out of her frail little body. I was not about to let the state or your father try and care for her in what was sure to be her last few months here on this earth.

The other life, well it was mine; mine to take any way I saw fit to do it. After the doctors knew that there simply was no other way around it, when we all knew I was a goner and in less than a few weeks I started to poison myself a little more each day, until I was forced into the hospital.

I wanted some time between my death and your eighteenth birthday. Why you ask? I want you to have a level head about what you do in the future. Don't stick with Annie and the beauty shop, unless you truly want to. I can't imagine why you would want to. Promise me, as you read this letter, you will think of yourself before anyone else and only do what you believe with all your heart you want to do!

Also promise me, you will find good memories of your Dad, Fratello, Sissy, and yes me, and hold on to them 'till you can replace them with better ones. Lord, I don't want to leave you. I wanted to see you dancing with your bride. I wanted you to have a ton of grandchildren for me to love on. Also, please, don't marry an Italian Jew because of your dad or me. Marry the true love of your life! I will miss you more than all the others.

Momma

Also Nic, as a parent you will learn you always hold out hope. If your brother should ever return, love on him like I have tried to love on you!

EPLOGUE

"Well, good morning. If I may ask, is it Nic, Nicky, what?"

"It's Nic, and thank you for asking. My mom and Tony, I'm sorry, Reuben, were the only ones who got away with calling me Nicky."

"It's okay, call him Tony. I know that's what you're used to. By the way, have you seen him this morning, I can't seem to find him anywhere?"

"Forgive me, but that's classic Tony for you. He is such a self-absorbed asshole!

"I'm sorry, I don't want to get into the middle of a brotherly disagreement, but you seem to, well, be somewhat upset with him."

"Yeah, and you should be too! He just took off with mom's car. Now he is well on his way up to the city."

"What city is that?"

"How much do you know about my brother?"

It didn't take Nic to long to see that either Tony had pulled the wool over poor Jimmy's eyes, or he had turned over a new leaf. Jimmy after all spoke as if Tony was a saint amongst saints.

"Let me put it to you like this, if I know my brother, like I think I do, he is stopping somewhere in Delaware for brunch right about now, and not giving you or I a second thought."

"Okay, my cousin and Tony work together at the park, and they both have joked with me about the fact that I can be a little naive at times."

"Forgive me, but Tony called someone else naive? There's a Yiddish word that makes me think of people like you. Oh God, I sound like my grandpa, but the word is schmuck. Some guys think with their schmuck, you know their little heads instead of using the big head, you know, the one on their shoulders. In other words, you're a fool to believe anything my brother tells you. I know way too much about your boyfriend to be anything but rude! Shit, I'll never make a good hairdresser. I'm way too honest, I haven't learned how to lie yet."

Jimmy practically jumped out of his chair as he asked, "Are you really a hairstylist?"

"Not really, why do you ask?"

"What, Tony never told you I'm a hairstylist?"

"Again, and please forgive me, but we really didn't have the time to sit and talk about everything under the sun. Hell, I just lost my sister and my mother; it's not your fault. It's just that I never thought he would come home for the funeral, Much less drag a stranger with him. I just wanted him to be able to say goodbye to her. You don't need to be dragged into our family's shit. My momma loved that boy and I loved my momma, and I would do anything for her. So, I moved heaven and earth to make sure the last thing she heard was his singing."

"Nic I believe in karma, and I just know in my heart something good is on its way to you."

"Is this real?"

"Is what real?"

"This Mr. Nice Guy thing you're doing."

It was over the breakfast table both Nic and Jimmy started to build a bond with one another.

"I mean, my brother has dragged you seven hundred miles from your home. He has left you sitting around with a bunch of crazy folks. I just told you he's gone three hundred and fifty miles north. I'll bet you dollars to doughnuts he's chasing down his old boyfriend.

And you just sit there with that stupid ass smile on your face. And you're not the least bit bothered! I'd want to kill him."

"Well, if what you said is true, yeah it hurts that Tony is looking for his old flame, but what can I do? I'll just pick up and move on."

"Wow, I wish I could learn how to be like that."

"Well Nic, to tell you the truth, when you're abused the way I was by your dad, you start to grow a little more calloused. Most of the time what people says to me goes in one ear and out the other. That part really comes in handy, when dealing with all the crazy clients in a salon."

"I could use someone with that mindset to teach me and some of the others in our salon."

"I'm sorry, but I thought you just said you're not a stylist."

"I'm not, but I manage a beauty shop."

As more time went on, Nic felt as if he had met his Gemini twin. Total opposite, yet totally the same.

"So, you always wanted to do hair?"

"Well, not really. My mom thought I should try for an office job. Could you see me in the steno pool or maybe accounting? I can do the adding and subtracting, but it's the multiplying and dividing that always gets the better of me!"

"You're sorta funny, in an odd way."

"Yeah, that would be me, you know what they say, all the world loves a clown. People come to the hairdresser as a cheap psychiatrist, they don't want to hear your problems, they just want to tell you about theirs."

"How long you been doing hair?"

"Let's see, I dropped out of school when I was fifteen, a year for school, and I'm now nineteen. So, two and a half years."

"How long do you want to do it?"

"Honestly, I can't think that far into the future, maybe 'till I get old. I don't know, maybe forty. Forgive me for asking, but I'd swear you had another reason for asking me all this. Nic, tell me more about the salon you manage?"

"Funny but I was just thinking about the styling salon."

"Nic, tell me this, if it was your salon, if you were the owner, what would you do with it?"

"Well, hell's bells as my dad would say, that's easy! If I have learned anything from one of my heroes, it's that doing the same thing and expecting a different outcome is insanity. Also, if you want the best out of an artist, make sure he or she has the tools needed to do the work you ask of them. Then just get the hell out of their way!"

#

"Who the hell would call at this ungodly hour on a Monday morning? Hello, this better be important!"

"So, I hear you're late for a very important date!"

"Who the hell is this?"

"It sure the hell isn't Merryweather, but I'd love to see him! I've come back from the pits of hell just to see you. Are you still at the same place?"

"Tony, oh my God, is that really you? Yeah, I'm at the same house, get your ass over here, hold on for just a..."

"Don't tell me old man, you have a guest over, and well, don't worry, I only have a very short window of time. It's not anyone I would know from the past, is it? I'm in your neighborhood and on my way over. I'll be there in just a few minutes!"

After only a minute of two Tony realized the smell of cologne along with the artwork on the walls seemed to be way to familiar. "Billy, I swear I have lost my mind, I miss him so much at times, I think I can smell him right now. Billy, please forgive me, but is Andy living here with you?"

"Yes, he is."

"Damn, I hit pay dirt, I found the two of you in one place. Is he here?"

"Yes, but Tony, he's not the same Andy. He doesn't want to see you. Tony, I love you like you were my very own child. Remember what he grew up in? He thinks the KGB is around each corner and under every rock. The night you two were separated, he stopped trusting anything. He fears you, well not you, but you being here in what's become his home.

I must say you do look good. Nice tan, but I don't know, I think it's the super short, extra light brown hair that's throwing me. It's nice to know you're alive. Tell me everything you can, without endangering yourself."

"Billy, you know me, wrong place, wrong time. I'm not sure what I can say, but I saw something and went to my Aunt Marie for some advice. The next thing I know, I have 72 hours to get all my shit together.

"Tony, I will always love you, but Andy and I are both in rehearsal, and we need to get into the city. I take it the trial didn't go well, or you would have moved back up to the city. Or did you find something or someone that's worth staying wherever you are at."

"Well, I'll let you two get going. As they say, break a leg."

"You don't need to rush off like that."

"Okay, so what's going on with the two of you?"

"Tony, how funny is this, but Billy is playing the part of Billy Flynn, the lawyer in "Chicago." I'm in this new show, "A Chorus Line." It's about a bunch of dancers going through the auditioning process. Really Tony, what are you doing with yourself nowadays?"

Just as Andy was beginning to ask his question of Tony, an alarm went off, letting everyone in the house know it was time to do something. Without saying a word, everyone knew it was Billy's paranoia prompting an early departure for the train station to head into the city. Tony reminded his two friends that he did have a car and could take them into the city.

He reassured them he could drive now, as learning was the first thing he had to do when he moved down south. As Tony pulled up to pay the toll for crossing under the East River via the Queens Midtown Tunnel, he was reminded of his Aunt Marie's warning. She warned him to never again enter into the city of Manhattan, for fear he may lose his life. As Tony drove his deceased mother's car in front of Bagel Stixs, Billy's favorite bodega on the corner of Fifty-Third and Eighth Avenue, he said his goodbyes to his two dear friends. As they walked away and into the store, he vowed to himself, that one day, he would come back to the city, regardless of the consequences. No, Tony didn't care anymore. What he needed to know more than anything was if there was any truth to the old saying, "You can always return home to the theatre."

#

"Good afternoon, thank you for calling Shear Delights, this is Annie, how may I help you?"

"This is Mrs. Snyder, I need to set an appointment. Is that young man Nic there, you know, he never messes up any of my appointments, like the rest of the girls do."

"Yes Mrs. Snyder, I couldn't agree more, Nic is practically perfect in every way imaginable."

"Yes he is. Did you say your name is Annie? Well, he is also very easy on the eyes, wouldn't you say?"

"Yes indeed, Mrs. Snyder he's just the most handsome 17-year-old boy I know. Mrs. Snyder, just think how much more attractive he might be if he was of age, you know, if he wasn't jailbait, younger than your own grandchildren. No, I'm afraid he won't be here that day. No, his mother will not be able to take you for a shampoo and set. I'm sorry to say this, but she is no longer with us. No, Mrs. Snyder, she wasn't fired, and no, she didn't quit either. Well, she passed away. Yes, Mrs. Snyder, young people do die occasionally. Yes, Mrs. Snyder, that's Thursday at 2:00 p.m. with Sally Ann for a shampoo and set. Yes, Mrs. Snyder, she knows how to tease hair properly. Yes, Mrs. Snyder, he'll be back on Friday. Yes, Mrs. Snyder, Sally will be around. Okay, we'll see you Friday morning at 10 o'clock. That's our only opening on Friday! Yes ma'am, if I get an opening at the last minute, for late Friday afternoon, yes ma'am, I'll call you. Yes ma'am, you have a nice day also."

"As long as she pays her bill, doesn't touch him, I don't care what she looks at!"

"You have got to be joking Annie, I thought you thought of Nic as a son."

"Oh, get real for just a second! I would be the first to take her down if I thought she would ever hurt that young boy. At the same time, we do have bills to pay."

"Is it really getting that bad around here?"

"Do you want the honest to God's truth?"

"Are we really that bad off?"

"Well, we won't be closing our doors tomorrow, but if something doesn't give soon, I'll be begging Dan to let me come over to his place and wait tables, that's for sure. Samantha, if some new, and I do mean new, talent doesn't show up in this little bitty town, Shear Delights might be saying good night."

THE END
The story continues in
Delilah's Legacy

About the Author

Mr. Cunningham resides in southeastern Virginia, with his two dogs. He still fantasizes of working at Walt Disney World, but he knows that ship has long since sailed. For many years people have told him to write a book. He has always said he was nothing more than a storyteller. At last he has made his attempt to transform one of his stories into a book.

One of Mr. Cunningham's favorite movies is *The Wizard of Oz* and he will tell you the best lines were delivered by Mrs. Margaret Hamilton, and had nothing to do with a dog. Without watching the movie he can hear her now, "These things must be done delicately," along with, "All in good time, all in good time." It is his life's goal to learn as much as he can about the writing of tall tales, and bring you his personal best! However, you must remember, these things must be done delicately, and yes, all in good time, all in good time.

Mr., Cunningham welcomes all your constructive critics. He can be found through the following links. He would also ask you to please help not only himself, but also all Indie Authors by leaving a review, wherever you purchased their works.

jondavidcunningham@gmail.com

http://www.jondavidcunningham.com

https://www.facebook.com/JonDavidCunningh amAuthor?ref=hl

http://www.amazon.com/Jon-David-Cunningham/e/B00FXW9DIU/ref=sr_tc_2_0?qid =1427903564&sr=1-2-ent

GLOSSARY

Russian
Bystra – quickly
Da – yes
Droug - friend
Durak – stupid
Mal'chik – male child
Moy – my
Nostrovia – A toast, "To your / our good health"
Privet - hello
Suka – bitch
Sumasshedshiy – crazy, silly
Ya lyublu tebya – I love you Tbi - you
Zhopa – butt, bum, ass

Yiddish
Bubbe – grandmother
Chutzpah –audacity, nerve, boldness
Mentsh – an upstanding gentleman
Mishegas – foolish, stupid
Ov - woe is me
Yenta - a busybody or gossip
Zaide – grandfather

Hebrew
Kaddish - Mourner's prayer
Messiah – The savior
Shabbat – A day of rest, the seventh day.
Shabbat Shalom - Sabbath of peace

Italian
Kapish – do you understand?
Fratello – brother

www.ingramcontent.com/pod-product-compliance
Lightning Source LLC
Chambersburg PA
CBHW071631140626
46555CB00022B/2211

* 9 7 8 0 9 8 8 8 8 9 7 0 5 *